BOOK 2 OF

BLUE FILM

KITTY KING

BLUE FILM

For information contact:

http://authorkittyking.com

Cover Design by Gemini Designs

Copyediting and Proofreading by Indie Proofreading

ASIN: B0C1R75ZK7 (eBook)

ISBN: (Paperback)

First Edition: January 2023

10 9 8 7 6 5 4 3 2 1

To those trapped under the weight of narcissistic relationships, may you be set free indeed.

author's note

This work of fiction contains content such as one scene of dubious consent with an underage protagonist and an older man and mentions forced body modification.

Full list of warnings can be found on my website at https://authorkittyking.com.

It helps to have read *Red Night,* the first book in the series, but this can be read as a standalone. Some events may seem rushed or out of place if not taken into context with Book 1.

childhood

ELLE

"Do you, Levi, take this woman to be your awful wedding wife?" Levi wasn't saying anything, just trying to drop my hands. His were sweaty, but I didn't mind. I kept hold of him even when my clover flower tiara fell in my face.

"You're not a woman. You're like a whole year younger than me. You're just a kid."

"Come on, Levi! You're 'sposed to say, 'I do'!" I squeezed his hands tighter.

Levi sighed loudly. "I do." He tried to shake off my hands again. "When do we get to the kissy part?"

"You want to kiss me?" My belly felt weird, like when my cousin Whitney and me had eaten too many gummy bears.

"Yeah, that's the whole point, isn't it? People get married to kiss whenever they want."

"Oh. I didn't know that." My mommy and daddy

1

didn't kiss each other. Maybe they didn't like to kiss. Daddy always went fishing, so his fingers smelled like the lake. That was probably why Mommy didn't want to kiss him. It would be kinda gross to kiss other boys in school. I thought I would like it if it were Levi who kissed me. "What about babies?"

"No! Babies smell bad and cry all the time." He rolled his eyes. "Can we just get to the kissy party now?" Levi shifted from one foot to the other, and I almost dropped the flowers I picked from Ms. Robinson's backyard. I hoped she didn't see me.

"I have to pronouns us... Mr. and Mrs. Joseph! Now, you may kiss me."

"Finally!" Levi leaned in and puckered his mouth. I puckered mine. He touched his lips to mine. It felt nice. I felt warm all over, and my cheeks got hot. He held there for a while. He said, "You are my first kiss, wife." Then he leaned in to do it again. I let him.

I liked Levi. He was the most handsome boy I had ever seen. Whenever Whitney and I played Barbies, I would always name my Ken doll "Levi" and have them get married. Levi had the same color hair as Ken.

Levi always smiled at me in school. He shared his Kit Kat candy bar with me once last year. Mommy would never let me have one. When I told him, he started to break off one piece for me each time he brought them.

"*Ew!*" Xavier Cardell rounded the tree with some

other boys from their class. The recess bell would ring soon. "Now you're gonna get some weird mouth disease!"

Levi shoved me away from him, and I fell to the ground. Mommy was going to be mad that my dress got dirty. He pointed at me and laughed, "Elle smells."

Xavier laughed and yelled, "That's her name! Smelly Ellie!"

The other boys started to laugh and yell, "Smelly Ellie! Smelly Ellie!"

The recess bell rang, and they ran off. I sat in the dirt and cried. Levi Joseph was mean, but I still wanted him to come back and kiss me again.

teen years

LEVI

I couldn't be the only one not to score. Xav kept bragging that he had made out with Katie Lane at the dance last year. I kept telling him I'd already made out with someone. He didn't know that Elle had been that someone in second grade. Chris and Kevin had no clue I hadn't gone as far as Xavier. I told them I'd felt up Sarah Anker after school one day, and they bought it. Xavier didn't. That jerkwad always knew when I was lying.

"You have to do it... and record it." Xavier smirked that stupid smile he always did. Chris and Kevin watched to see what I would do.

"I will. I will. No problem. Done it before. Relax." I looked around the room. We were in the basement of Trent Dunn's house for the middle school graduation party. I couldn't go into high school without sticking my tongue into a girl's throat. Or feeling a boob.

He could pick Joy Bennett. She was super uptight. I wouldn't be able to get my tongue past her lips. Or maybe she'd let me just so she could bite it off.

Yuck. What if he chose that girl with the weird thing on her face over by the food table? I forgot her name; she was creepy. She looked like that girl from *The Ring*.

Whitney Ward and some other popular girls were dancing in front of the TV. Xavier wouldn't pick any of them for sure. Whitney was hot, but I wondered if her being here meant that she came with... *Yes*! There she was. Elle Townsend, her cousin.

Elle was only in seventh grade, but I'd had a crush on her since that day behind the oak tree at recess. She looked different this year. She had big glasses and braces now, but, *man*, I still thought she was totally cute. It even looked like she was wearing a bra now. Hmm, maybe A cups?

I heard Xavier snicker. "I got it... Smelly Ellie. You have to make out with *that*," he said as he pointed to Elle standing near her cousin. Chris and Kevin started cackling, repeating her ridiculous nickname. Ha! Xavier fell for it. She was exactly the girl I wanted him to pick.

"Ugh, really, dude?" I pretended to be disgusted. I wouldn't win if they knew I enjoyed it.

The guys bet twenty dollars each that I couldn't make out for ten minutes with a girl and touch her boobs to prove I'd done it before. All because I ran my mouth, and Xav had to call me on it. I could feel myself getting closer to that new Madden game... "Fine. I'll get her to do it." Xavier started to open his mouth, but I continued, "—and record it."

I strolled over to Whitney and her friends. Elle kept her eyes on me as I made my approach. Whitney stopped dancing and smiled. The clique of girls stared at me as if I were an alien visiting their home planet. I almost gagged at the cotton candy scent that hit my nose.

"Hey, Whit. You like this song?" I flashed her the smile I knew worked to get me out of trouble with teachers, my mom (when she had been around), and all the girls in eighth grade. Whitney giggled and touched my arm; she had an ugly gold tennis bracelet on her wrist that had to be expensive.

I glanced at Elle, who was staring at me with her big blue eyes, accentuated in their size by how thick her glasses were. Hmm, I'd have to take those off.

"Yeah! You wanna dance—"

Before she would ask, I interrupted, "Oh, I see you brought your cousin. What's her name?"

"Oh, she's no one. She's just a seventh grader."

What a bitch. "Heh, just a seventh grader." I turned to little Elle. Her eyes got even wider; she looked terrified. "Well, seventh grader, you ever play a game called Seven Minutes in Heaven?"

"I have!" Whitney jumped in. "Do you want to play?" She grabbed my arm.

"Do *you*?" I turned to Elle and asked. The girl looked like she might pass out. Her pale skin got even more ashen, and her light eyes faded. She looked like a fragile doll.

"Uh, play with you?" Elle barely spoke above a whisper, but her voice made me want to lean into her to hear her better.

"Yeah... Come on, dollface." I grabbed Elle's little hand and pulled her to Trent's room. "Yo! Trent. I gotta use your bedroom for a bit, man!" Trent and some of the other guys started shouting and whooping.

Trent said, "There he goes again." I had made a reputation for myself with all my lies.

Xavier held up his phone and shook it in the air. I nodded.

After closing and locking the door, I led Elle over to the bed. She eased herself onto the edge gingerly.

"Wha—what is this game?" she asked.

"Oh, it's fun. You'll like it." I put my phone on Trent's dresser, facing Elle, propped against a tissue box. "I'm gonna turn on some music." I turned on an R&B playlist and hit the record button on the camera. I walked over and sat next to Elle on the squishy mattress. Trent's bed was unmade, and he had too many basketball posters in his room. The place smelled like sweat.

Elle asked, "What do we do?"

"You ever made out with anyone before?"

8

"No. I mean, not since..." She was searching my face to see if I remembered our kiss.

Sliding her glasses off, I could see her eyes better. Her hair was the color of the sunlight on a winter morning. She had cream skin dotted with freckles along her button nose. Now that I could see them, her eyes were less blue and more of a pale green shade, like the jade rings my mother used to wear. I gazed at her rose-colored, full bottom lip. Her wide cupid's bow was pushed out by her buck teeth covered in clear braces. Those could cause a problem. I took a breath. "You never kissed anyone... after that, I mean."

"N-no." She was staring at me as much as I was staring at her. It made all the blood rush from my head to my other head. That could be embarrassing if she noticed.

"Do you want to?" I glanced down at her chest. It was small, but she was just a seventh grader. I could make out the outline of a bra, maybe one of those made with silk. I wondered what color it was.

Elle glanced at my crotch. Shit, she was looking at my dick. Well, now it was a full boner in my pants. Her cheeks flushed to the color of her lips.

"Yes."

There were about ten minutes before Xavier or one of the guys would do something irritating to interrupt me. I didn't want them to know how into this girl I was. I would never hear the end of it if I dated "Smelly Ellie." Nor did I want to. Elle was too young. High school girls put out. Soon I'd be moving on from childish middle school make-out parties and be able to get my dick wet.

Weaving my hand through Elle's white-gold hair and wrapping it around the back of her neck, I brought us closer, lips almost touching. She inhaled quickly, and I could smell some fruit like mango. My mind flashed back to the day we had our fake wedding at recess. Her scent was so tasty that I wanted to eat her. Back then, I couldn't let Xavier know, so I pushed her and said she "smelled" when he caught us.

I pretended I knew what I was doing up until this point. Reality hit, and I realized how out of my league I was. This was the point I always froze when alone with a girl. Maybe I could run out of the room and tell Xavier, Chris, and Kevin to screw themselves. No, I'd never live it down. Everyone knew we were in the bedroom together.

"Are—are you going to kiss me, Levi?"

The way her tongue hit the back of her teeth as she said my name made my erection jump in my pants. She wanted this. I leaned in and lightly sucked on her mouth, then pulled back. But I couldn't stop.

I jammed my lips to hers. With her braces in the way, it hurt, but I shoved my tongue in and scraped her teeth, anyway. She did taste like mangoes. I wanted to suck on her to get more flavor in my mouth.

Why was there so much drool? Didn't she know how to swallow? We bumped foreheads, and it was so painful that we both reared back.

"Ouch!" she yelled. She took her hand and wiped her chin from drool. I did the same.

"Sorry." I went in again, this time with less tongue-punching. She tried to pull back because our noses were in the way. I tilted my head more. We began full-on making out, our tongues dancing with each other, tip to tip, flittering around our mouths. I was doing it; it was working! I kept tugging back to swallow spit so there wasn't as much drool. Then I would dive back in and kiss her more. She tasted so sweet that I sucked on her tongue.

Now I just had to go for the holy grail. I withdrew my hand from her hair and placed it on her stomach. Her little hand covered mine but didn't stop me from moving. She wore a pink ruffled top, and I crawled my fingers underneath it. I felt her suck in a breath in my mouth. "What are you doing?"

"Just want a feel of your perfect body, hotness." Inching my fingers up her flat stomach, I found the bottom of her bra. I was right; it was silky.

Her thighs clenched together in her little cotton shorts. I would explode in my jeans if she even peeped at my crotch again. My forehead touched hers as I cupped her little tit in my palm. I kissed her again, and she moaned in my mouth. Oh, man... I just needed to relieve a little pressure.

With the hand leaning behind us, I grabbed her fingers and positioned them around my boner. She gasped and tried to yank her hand back. I held her there so she couldn't and pumped into it. I nodded at her that it was okay to keep going and kissed her quickly before she would say anything. I curled my other fingers inside her bra and felt her tiny, hard nipple.

"Levi!" she said into my mouth with shock.

That was all it took. I pumped one more time in her hand and came in my boxers with a loud groan. I forced her hand on my dick and kept humping it, kept coming, making a huge mess in my jeans. Shit, Xavier would never let me live this down. Maybe he wouldn't notice.

Pulling my hands back, I adjusted myself. Maybe I could cover the spot up with something? "Ugh, sorry, dollface. Couldn't help myself. You're just so hot." I flashed my smile.

"It's okay. We can—we can kiss more if you want." She appeared hopeful.

Just then, I heard Trent yell, "Alright, mother-fucker! Time's up!" He banged loudly on the door.

"Alright, alright!" I yelled back. "This was fun," I told Elle as I got up. I did want to stay and make out more, but I couldn't let the guys know. Plus, my lips felt chapped.

I grabbed my phone and stopped recording. Elle stood up, and I strode over to her. I put my hands through her hair and inhaled deeply to memorize her fruity scent to jerk off to later. I kissed her on the lips, no tongue this time. "See you around, hotness."

Stretching my T-shirt down as much as I could, I hid my cum stain. When I opened the door, all the guys were crowded around it as if they'd been listening. Most of them were laughing. Some patted my back.

Whitney and the other girls flipped their hair and turned their backs in a display of loyalty to their leader. A few looked at me as if they wanted a turn with me. I wanted to go back into the room with Elle.

"Alright, hand it over. Let's see the evidence," Xavier said above the crowd. I pulled out my phone and loaded the video, fast-forwarding to the point I was up her shirt and her hand was on my crotch. We looked good together. The video was hot. I stopped it and put my phone back in my pocket. They didn't need to see all of it. I'd save it for when I was alone.

Chris reached out without a word and handed me a crisp twenty-dollar bill. Kevin did the same. I took the money, and Xavier crossed his arms. "Well, I guess you earned it. No one would wanna make out with Smelly Ellie, poor guy," he said loudly. He dramatically handed me some cash with a fake half-bow and his signature smirk. I wanted to hit him, but before I did, I heard a sob behind me.

Elle was standing in the doorway. She had obviously heard him. Pushing through the crowd, she ran up the basement steps crying. The guys started cackling harder. I was going to kill Xavier. If I did, though, he'd know. He'd know how I felt about her.

So I laughed with them.

Boys are stupid; I'd learned this from a young age. It was the only thing my mother ever told me that was right. The single exception to this rule was my father, who was perfect in every way. No one could compare.

Despite the absurdity of the opposite sex, I couldn't stop myself from wanting penis all the time. It was my life's curse. Be a slave to stupid penis and what one has to do to get it. That included heading to the Delta fraternity party.

I didn't enjoy parties as much as people thought I did. It was just how one with a stupid penis fetish had to troll for fish. And that night, dressed in my lacy aqua halter top and black pleather skirt, I hoped to hook a big one.

More so than reeling one in, I enjoyed the tease, the chase. I was a flirt, and everyone knew it. People assumed I was a "slut" in high school. The football team said they had been with me, and so had the soccer team. The baseball team added their input in the spring. The basketball team in the winter... There were a lot of guys that claimed I had slept with them or had given them head. It was all untrue.

When I felt a boy snag my lure, I wanted to cut the line. The victory lay in knowing he desired me. Then, I could walk away. I wasn't a virgin by any stretch, but I also wasn't as experienced as some would believe. When I was with a boy, I let things get only so far before retreating, that powerful feeling keeping me full when I did.

The same was not true for *men*, however. Older guys were much less stupid than high school or university boys. They knew what they were doing.

My first time was with one of my dad's finance associates. It was at a pool party we held at our house every year. It was the summer before my junior year in high school. I had just turned sixteen and had a crush on Brad since he visited us for dinner when he joined my dad's company.

Brad was fit and good-looking. He had just graduated with his Master's in business, and I found out from his social media that he was twenty-five and single. From a beach vacation picture he posted, I also saw what an amazing body he kept under his white button-downs. I knew if he worked for my father, he would be rich, which was the most important thing, according to Veronica Townsend.

I assumed my mother had set us up when he came over for dinner the first time; Brad was the kind of man she would pick for me. She always reminded me that Emilia and Elizabeth were already dating a pre-med and a cousin of a Kennedy, respectively. Fortunately, my older sisters were already away at college, so I was down to one puppet master instead of three.

The pool party was the annual highlight for William Townsend's financial planning company, littered with businessmen cutting loose from their daily grind. No kids were allowed, so I was ordered to stay out of sight, even though I was of legal age in our state (I'd checked). I decided to peek my body out to catch a glimpse of Brad while dressed in my tiniest bikini, making the excuse that I couldn't find my phone.

After I spotted him, and he *definitely* spotted me, I turned with a look over my shoulder and went into the kitchen for a drink. My trap set, he followed me inside, asking for the bathroom. I moved closer to him to point out where it was, almost touching my body to his. He grabbed me by the shoulders and stuck his tongue down my throat.

"How old are you now?" He breathed into my mouth.

"Seventeen," I lied.

"*Damn*, you look older than that. Could be like

twenty-one." His gaze was intense as he searched my body to see if something was hidden in last year's swimsuit.

I knew I had grown since the previous summer, and boys took notice. Gone were the days of my braces and glasses; I had contacts and straight teeth. My mother insisted I get breast implants "for men" once she realized I wouldn't be as full as my sisters. I didn't mind; my cleavage was the perfect bait.

"I think this bathroom down here is broken. There's one upstairs next to my room. I could show you if you want."

"Oh, you could, could you?" Brad narrowed his eyes and kissed me again. He was a bit rough, but he was a man. He was older, and he knew what he was doing.

I led Brad by the hand to my bedroom, prepared to show him the ensuite. As soon as we entered, he shut and locked my door. Suddenly, he was all over me. He untied my bikini quickly while kissing me, hands clutching my bare breasts. "Fuck, you're so hot." I giggled, not knowing exactly what to say.

He laid me back on the bed and slid his hands up my thighs while kissing my neck. "You won't tell your dad, right?"

"N-no. I won't tell."

He began to finger me harshly and, feeling how wet I was, tugged his swim trunks off. His was the first penis I had seen in the flesh and not online. It was kind of scary: big, red, and sticking straight out at me. He began to masturbate, but it was like strangling his dick with his hand.

"You ever done this before?" He knelt over my body.

I didn't exactly know what he was talking about—done what before? Been naked with one of my dad's employees in my bedroom? No.

I didn't want Brad to think I was inexperienced. He was so cool and older. Whatever he was going to give me, I wanted. He could be my door out of this dollhouse.

"Yeah, lots of times," I said with confidence that I did not feel.

Brad snorted. "Okay, sexy." He slid his body on top of mine, pulling my knees up, so my core was exposed and wide open for him. He hovered above me, his lips almost kissing mine again. "You said eighteen, right?"

I was dazed with lust, wanting that kiss again. "Yeah, eighteen..."

Brad pushed inside of me roughly, and I cried out in pain. "Fuck, that's too tight! What the—you said you'd done this before!" Brad was pulling back out of me, blood covering his penis and my thighs. I sat up to look between us. He had broken me! Was that supposed to happen? Did I need to go to the emergency room? Did I get my period? Veronica would be so mad. I flushed with embarrassment.

I sniffed through tears, "Um... I'm so sorry. I'm so, so sorry!"

"*Damn it*! Just lay back. Gotta nut." Brad covered my mouth with his hand and pumped inside of me with more force. The pain quickly changed from pressure to pleasure, and I knew I wanted to do this with him again as soon as possible. Knowing this man would help me escape my prison, I came on his dick, and he briefly glanced at me and grinned. I felt so connected to him at that moment. He slowed his thrusts before picking back up again. Brad groaned loudly, and his body shuddered. He hung his head next to mine on the bed, panting to catch his breath.

"Hey, that was great. You're really fucking hot." Brad stood up and pulled up his shorts. He tapped a kiss on my lips and then walked to my bedroom door. He stopped and said, "Remember... don't tell your dad." He smiled at me before walking out.

I was lying on the bed, thighs covered in blood, leaving a stain on the comforter. I would have to hide it from Veronica. Although, she would probably be okay with it if she knew I was dating an MBA.

After hiding my bedding and putting on a fresh set of sheets, I cleaned up and waddled back downstairs. The pain between my legs was noticeable. Brad never looked at me for the rest of the party and left without saying a word. I kept waiting for him to come back or call me. I don't think he lasted a year at Dad's company.

His quick departure from my room only heightened my obsession with him. I stalked him on social media for three years. *Okay*, I still occasionally checked it. He now had a wife and a kid. But why didn't he want me?

The day after he took my virginity, I got scared I would get pregnant. Fortunately, I never did. The fear was enough to have me sneak to a clinic after school and get some birth control. I also hid condoms in every bag I owned.

My sexual experiences declined in quality following my first. The two high school boys I had sex with didn't last long. I slept with three university boys whose names I forgot before they even came.

I was heading to a Delta party with the understanding that I would be disappointed if I aimed for some magical sexual experience. It was much more fun to catch and release. Then I could get myself off with my new purple dildo waiting back in my dorm room once my roommate was asleep.

Sporting my six-inch leopard print stilettos, I tried not to trip over the steps of the fraternity house as I approached. I arrived alone, knowing I was on the prowl. It never worked out when I brought someone with me to parties. Not that I had many friends. Girls looked at me like I'd steal their boyfriend. Or they wanted to travel in a pack like a beaver dam. Guys only wanted under my skirt.

Marissa was the one friend I had met at university

(so far), but she was probably with her new boyfriend, James. I had set them up; I was good at that... for everyone except myself. My dormmate had made it clear there was to be no "partying" anywhere near our room, so I didn't bother to invite her along. It wasn't a big deal; I had tons of acquaintances on campus and would probably run into someone I knew inside.

The party was insanely packed. People spilled out onto the front lawn, the backyard, the porches, and the windows up on the second story. Bass bumps were felt more than heard as I stepped through the front door.

"Whoa!" A few boys leered at me as I entered; I ignored them. Not my kind of fish. The Delta who had approached me for an invite came down the stairs as I was contemplating where to go. He saw me and grinned.

"Hey! You came," he said, and I smiled back. He was cute. Probably a senior. My flirt target for the night had been acquired.

"Yeah, hey. Thanks for the invite."

"I'm Cody, by the way. I forgot to catch your name." He was leading me out of the doorway to a kitchen area with a wave of his hand.

"I'm Elle."

"Hot name. Goes with your body." I cringed. Maybe he wouldn't be the target. "Want a drink?" Cutting the line to the keg, he poured me a plastic cup of foamy beer, then one for himself. No one in the queue said anything when he went first. At least he had respect among the heathens.

"Thanks," I said, sipping the watery suds.

Cody attempted his best to engage in an intelligent conversation. Well, it was less a conversation than it was him trying to prove to me how smart he thought he was. He was a philosophy major; I was bored within two minutes. He kept staring at my D cups, which meant I had him, but it was too easy. There was no fun in this game. I kept drinking the beers until I was buzzed enough not to care.

"Yo! Cardell!" Cody finally stopped his soliloquy to speak with someone behind me as we stood in the corner of the kitchen. Hearing that name made me feel like an insecure little girl with glasses and braces again. I didn't turn around.

"Yo, Meyer, what's up?" Xavier Cardell walked around me to fist-bump Cody. Xavier eyed my chest without a glimpse at my face.

"Want a beer, man? I'll grab you one." Cody went to get another beer, but the keg was tapped, so he headed out the back door while Xavier lifted his eyes to mine. He stood there for a moment, trying to figure me out with his intense gaze. I wanted to run and hide from the boy who could transport me back to some of my worst moments.

"You Meyer's girl, or what?"

He didn't recognize me. How self-centered was he? "No."

He smirked. "Yeah? You alone here, then?" I supposed that look made panties wet, but I knew what an asshole he was. He stopped himself before making his next move. "Wait! Wait..." My stomach was tied in a knot, and I wanted to disintegrate into a black hole. "Smelly Ellie? *Holy shit,* you grew up. Oh... damn. Wait until Levi sees you."

At the mention of Levi Joseph, I almost vomited all the soapy beer onto Xavier's expensive Italian loafers. It would serve him right. What kind of person wore those shoes to a fraternity party anyway?

"Uh, I go by 'Elle' now." I tried to sound superior and not like I wanted to rip his head off. These types of bullies thrived on that kind of stuff.

"Oh, hey... I've seen you around campus with your friend, Marissa?"

"Yeah. Marissa and I are friends." Was he going to make fun of her, too? He better back the fuck off. I'd kick his ass.

"Is she from around here? Do you know her dad's name?" He seemed overly interested. If I talked to her, I'd have to let her know.

"Sorry, I don't know her that well—"

"—Yo! Check who it is, Lev!" I squinted my eyes closed at the approaching footsteps.

"*Daaaamn*, that looks like my next lay... What do you say? Want to hit the hay?" An arm was thrown over my shoulder, and a very inebriated Levi Joseph hung from it, huffing stale beer into my face.

I tried to shuck off his arm. "What's your name, hotness?"

Oh, so he called every girl that. And, of course, he doesn't remember me. "'Ima Toohot.'"

"Ima Toohot?"

"Yeah, I'm too hot for you." I shoved him off me as he and Xavier laughed. Xavier slinked away to help Cody with the new kegs.

"Wait, you're Elle Townsend! Well, well, well. Look at little Elle all grown up..." Levi slurred every word as his eyes were glued to my breasts. Why did he have to look so *good*? Even when wasted and obnoxious, I wanted to ride his face.

He had filled out since middle school. Muscles were everywhere, and his tight T-shirt did nothing to hide them underneath. He wasn't too bulky nor too lean. His wavy, light brown hair was perfectly styled imperfectly. His golden brown eyes were bloodshot, probably from being high. His wide jaw was covered by just a slight bit of fuzz, enough to make him look less like a pretty boy and more like a rugged man, especially with his prominent Adam's apple that I couldn't keep my eyes from.

"Yep. And little Levi grew up to be a mess. No surprises there."

"What do you mean, a mess? I'm not that drunk. Could still fuck you raw all night, twelve rounds. Let's go." He put his arm around me again and tried to tug me away.

"Ew. No thanks. I don't do guys that come in their jeans before we ever get started." I shoved him off me again.

Levi's jaw dropped as he gasped. "Don't say that... Oh, come on, dollface. That was rude."

"Well, so's your face." I glared at him. "I regret that we have to be at the same university. I would have gone out of state if I'd known."

"You still mad after all these years?"

"Levi, seriously?" I couldn't let on how pissed off I was about their old prank; he'd probably use it to make fun of me.

"If it's worth anything, I'm sorry. I wanted to go down on you at Trent's house." He leaned in to murmur in my ear, "Want me to make up for it now?"

Fortunately, Cody came to claim me. "This guy bothering you?"

"Yes. Take me somewhere safe." I flittered my eyelashes at Cody. He bought it.

"Time to sober up, man," Cody said to Levi like he was a disobedient child. He wrapped his arm around me and led me from the kitchen.

"Whore!" I heard Levi yell at my back as we left.

I turned, kissed the tip of my fingers, and waved goodbye to him.

O f course, I knew who she was. Why did I have to be so sloshed when she saw me again? *Damn.* Thought I'd throw some game, flash the smile, and finally get to fuck Elle Townsend. Xavier even played the ultimate wingman, distracting that douche she was with so I could talk to her. Set me up perfectly, and I struck out. Then threw a tantrum in rejection. Aces.

Elle had grown up, *really* grown up. Amazing body: huge tits, round ass, long legs, blond hair... Mmm, just my type. She always did look good, though. I could still see some of the shy, cute, freckled girl behind the hot chick vibe she had going on.

Oh, well. Didn't matter. I'd find some other hot co-ed and hook up with her. It was good to keep options open. Elle was the girl I would have feelings for, and I couldn't do that. Wouldn't do that. Girlfriends, wives,

27

and *relationships* were bullshit designed to fail. Monogamy was a trap. I still did want to fuck her. Just once.

Instead, I went home alone with a whiskey dick.

The day after the Delta party, I had to jump through my father's latest hoop of the week: a golf outing with him and my older brother, Adam. I didn't care about the game. I wasn't any good at it, which disappointed my father. I'd go, though, because disappointing my father was my favorite pastime.

Warren Joseph was Chief Financial Officer of Cardell Enterprises, the company that owned most of the town and had its hands in the pockets of everyone who mattered. Father was overly involved in my life in a detached sort of way. He was only interested in facts that made him look good or that he could share with his friends at cocktail parties when they asked, "How's your son?"

I had to study finance because he studied finance. We had to golf together because we would be seen. He controlled every part of my life. How could I resist? I was at his mercy. My tuition, my name, my reputation, my future... it all belonged to Warren Joseph.

Not only was I cursed with a narcissist for a father, but I was doomed with a hysteric for a mother. When she left us for her tennis instructor, I held a sad debate on which breeder to live with. My mother said I was too "wild" for her to manage and refused to take me with her, making my choice easy.

Since seventh grade, every time I visited her was torture. I couldn't stand Ted, her husband, and their annoying brood of brats. I didn't consider them my siblings, just as I didn't consider her a mother.

One thing I did admire about Warren was that he chose never to remarry. He had taken some models or well-known women from the community to company events, but did not seriously date anyone. I was pretty sure he was a devout celibate. Too virtuous for tainting his cock with anyone except those with a safety seal still attached to their pussy. Father didn't want a relationship; he wanted to be worshipped.

My reprieve from a life devoid of tender loving care had been my brother Adam. Older by two years, he'd had enough experience to expertly keep the heat off when Warren would lay into me. Adam got away with a lot; I was often told, "no excuses." Adam chose to stay with Father when our mother abandoned us, and I've wondered if that's why Warren never cut me any slack.

We arrived at the course as a family, almost matching in our pastel Polo shirts and khaki pants. We were meeting Xavier and his father, Malcolm Cardell, and Xavier's cousin, Mason Locke. The Cardells were my second family growing up; Xavier's father was like one I'd never had.

Xavier was the only one who could understand my life. He was expected to lead his father's company once he earned his MBA. Xavier handled expectations better than I did. Whereas I wanted to be left alone, Xavier took his role as heir seriously. Maybe it was because I was the youngest. I dreamed that Adam would take over for Father, but he was in law school. That meant I was deemed to be the successor in the company.

"S'up, dudes." I greeted my two friends.

"Man, you missed it after you left, you louse." Mason always had some story to tell, usually one devoid of any couth.

Xavier rolled his eyes. "Just concentrate on not hitting the sand today."

"What happened?" I asked, knowing I would probably regret it. Xavier gave me a look that let me know I would.

"Man, you know the Delta president—what's his name, Cory?"

"Cody," Xavier interrupted, inspecting his clubs. Our fathers were behind us with Adam. Caddies were running up to grab our bags.

"Yeah, Cody. Anyway, I saw him last night before we left the party. The dude was railing some chick's ass on top of one of the kegs. Right over the tap! Fortunately, it was empty." Mason had that foolish open-mouth grin he got after telling some asinine story; I wanted to slap it off. Xavier gazed at me and shook his head once. Mason was serious as he asked, "You think that was his way of announcing last call?"

"Locke, you gonna talk all day or hit the ball?

You're up." Xavier interrupted his little storytelling session. I pretended to clean a club, put on my gloves, anything so they wouldn't notice my frustration.

I'd heard the rumors. My brother was dating her cousin, and I'd overhear Whitney gossiping about Elle. Whitney would act like some pious leader trying to help her wayward servant return to the fold. I knew Elle liked to get down; I could appreciate a girl that loved to fuck... I just wished it was with me.

Xavier bent to tie his shoe in front of me. Quietly, so Locke wouldn't hear, he said, "It wasn't her."

I pretended I didn't hear him, but relief flooded my body. "Huh?" I kept looking down so he wouldn't see my face.

Xavier stood to walk away and said with a barely audible voice, "It was some other girl."

Yes! I felt a weird sort of victory, like I had preserved some of Elle's innocence. Innocence I likely ruined back in eighth grade. Elle's ass belonged to me in some way. She just didn't know it yet.

After a horrible round, Xavier taking the pot as usual, we headed to the restaurant for lunch. The clubhouse was the male version of a knitting circle. Most business gossiping (they called it "networking") took place there.

It was often a struggle to make it to a table. We rolled in like local celebrities, and adoring fans interrupted our group every few steps. The university football coach was there with the

31

athletic director; they were the most important guests, so that took some of the attention off us. Mal and my father were runners-up for most popular.

"Great to see you again, Adam. Heard you were interning with Steven Smith, but we plan to snag you from them if you try to sign." Some fancy lawyer was talking to my brother. The man turned to my father. "What about your youngest? Levi, is it? Is he... Oh well, here he is!" On cue, I did my smile.

My father put his arm around me as if he liked me. "Levi is studying finance in his second year. He plans to get his MBA with Cardell's son after graduation. Then he'll be helping me in my role. What did you get last semester, Levi? Straight As? Made the Dean's List. He's also a member of Theta Rho Zeta fraternity." The lawyer pretended to be impressed, then tried to one-up Warren with his own progeny tales.

I answered inane questions and made chatty comments when there was a pause in the conversation. My role was to be a quiet, well-behaved younger son that hadn't blasted cum into the daughters of half the men in the room. Adam talked more about his internship, saving me from wanting to burst into flames. Finally, we made it to our seats and ordered food.

"Well, I know it's been a while since we were all together, so I wanted to announce that I plan to propose to Whitney next week." Adam appeared proud. I felt sick.

Mal breathed out a loud congratulatory yell, "Well done!"

"Couldn't be prouder of you, son," my father said and clapped him on the back.

Xavier shoveled his sandwich in his mouth while keeping his eyes on me. Mason said, "I don't think I'll ever get married. Tied to one pussy? Nah."

Xavier snorted. "Locke, you can't even pull one." I knew what he was doing. He was trying to distract me so I wouldn't say what I was about to.

"That's a stupid mistake." I looked at Adam. My dad and Mal stopped eating. Adam looked down as if he expected me to say this, "She's a complete bitch."

"Levi!" my father bellowed.

"What? Adam knows it. Maybe you even like it." I shook my head. "You'll regret it."

Adam wasn't angry. He said, "I know you guys don't get along. Hopefully, you can learn to." Adam elbowed my father, who looked like he may have had a stroke. "Dad, it's fine. It'll be fine." Adam's face was soft as he grimaced and said, "You're not going to lose your big brother."

How did he do that? Just that one sentence shut everyone up. He knew I was worried about losing him to anyone, especially to such a controlling cunt.

Adam's statement also shut my father's mouth, eyes now filled with pride, gazing upon his eldest son.

I knew Adam would regret marrying her. However, it was his own mistake to make. Unless I could get Locke and Xavier to help me hide her body some-where... I glanced up at Xavier, but he shook his head as if reading my mind.

Whitney Ward was the devil. She was just like my mother. Maybe it was some weird Oedipal thing Adam had going on. They'd only been together a year. Adam was trying to marry a society girl, but she would make him miserable. I just knew it.

Given that horrible news, I knew what I was doing that night. Or *who* I would do that night. I hated to repeat pussy after a terrifying experience in high school.

Big George Turner ("Big G" we called him) was having a party our senior year. He caught Xavier and me in a foursome with his stepmother and stepsister in the guest room. Later, Mason spilled that I had been with them a few times already throughout our senior year. Big G rarely spoke, so when he got up and yelled, it was enough to scare the shit out of me. Since then, I liked *one and done*s.

My exception was a woman named Samantha, whom my father often took to events. She had just turned forty, and even at twenty years my senior, she looked just as good or better than many of the girls I was in class with. She never had any drama and didn't care that I didn't spend the night. She didn't want anything more. She knew what she wanted and loved sex. Every time I would plunge into her, I could feel my father's disappointment rising, making me come so much harder than I did with other women.

I pulled out my phone and texted her under the table to see if she was busy that evening. The reply was immediate:

MILF SAM

Always have time for you, cutie.

Sweet. She was always craving my cock. I liked pussy on demand.

As I looked up, Will Townsend was approaching our table. His plastic wife walked behind him, but no Elle. Briefly, sadness flashed through me. I ignored it.

"Cardell and Joseph! Good to see you both." The two stood, shaking hands with the newcomer.

"Would you and Veronica care to join us? We can make room. Here." Mal moved some chairs closer to the table.

"Oh, Mal, you're always so kind. Thank you for the invitation. I'll be dining with the girls before our Bridge game." Veronica ran a hand down Xavier's father's arm. Xavier tilted his head to the side and stared at me. All of us knew what a cuck Veronica had made of her husband. The only one who didn't was Will himself. Not that Mal would fall for her antics. He moved away from her touch slyly. Will hadn't noticed a thing.

Veronica walked back to her "girls," the wives of

important men within our community. Will sat down with us. I always liked Will. One of my daydreams had been to work in trades for his company once I graduated. It would be the ultimate insult to Warren Joseph.

"How's your game been, Townsend?" my father addressed Will.

"Oh, terrible. Haven't been playing much. Just came to drop Veronica off for lunch. See who's here." Will always seemed to be smiling. I could see where Elle got her eye color and demeanor... when she wasn't trying to be snarky.

"Oh? What have you been up to?" Mal pitched in.

"I fish. Down at Gold Bottom Creek. Take my youngest there every Saturday morning when I can."

"So, not a boat fisherman then," my father said, curling his lip. I could tell he was disgusted by even thinking of an activity so pedestrian.

Will chuckled. "Nah. We like to get in there for the bass. Sometimes trout. Minnows."

Mason said, "Oh, I've been catfishing there a few times with my dad." Xavier glanced at me, and we both smiled at the joke we could make at Mason's expense if not for our fathers' presence.

Will nodded. "Yeah, there're a few spots that we like around the back cove." He ordered his food as I tried to picture beautiful, blond Elle standing in a creek with pigtails and fishing waders casting a rod. I reached down subtly to adjust my dick in my khakis.

Will continued, "Adam, you must be close to graduating now. Entering your last year in law?"

"Yes, sir." Adam smiled politely. "Interning with Smith and Goldstein now. Is Elizabeth enjoying her first year with Weiss and Guzman?"

"Oh, yes. She's been very happy there."

"Must be short in the pockets planning that wedding to Weiss' son. I heard he has expensive tastes." My father shook his head. "Three girls... couldn't imagine."

Mr. Townsend laughed. "Yes, it would have been cheaper to have sons." Turning to the Cardells, he said, "Xavier, you still planning to take over for your father? He'll need your help." He winked at Mal. Mal chuckled.

"Yes, sir. I can't escape." Xavier smirked. Oh, how true that statement was. We didn't even need to look at each other to feel our understanding.

"And Levi. It's been a while. Heard you were studying finance like your father." He took a sip of his scotch. "You enjoying it?"

My own father had never once asked me if I enjoyed something. It made me pause, wondering if I should honor Will with the truth or save myself the hassle on the drive home later. "Yes! Thinking of doing trades... I'm mainly into crypto right now." My father's face crinkled.

"Oh! Well, we are always looking for new traders

with a good eye on things. Can't wait to see what your future holds."

"Now, now, Will. Trying to steal my next CFO?" Mal joked to lighten the tension we all could feel from my father's side of the table.

The rest of the lunch was a bit quieter. After we said our goodbyes and got into my father's Mercedes, I leaned my head against the headrest, knowing what was about to unfold.

"Do you find entertainment embarrassing me?" My father backed out of the club's parking lot.

"Yes," I said without inflection. He stopped the car.

"Should I stop your tuition payments?"

"I don't know, maybe." My mind flashed to a vision of myself on an island beach, writing poetry in a lounge chair. Elle was lazily sucking my cock after I read her some beautiful words. Then we were taking fish back from the ocean to a dilapidated apartment with peeling painted plaster to fry up our catch for dinner, but we'd make love before it was finished.

"Father, he's just messing around. Besides, it's good experience for him and a great business venture *on the side* as he's finishing his undergrad." Adam turned on talk radio. "Cardell Enterprises could look into crypto companies more... Oh, I meant to get your opinion. Whitney said she wanted a destination wedding. I thought that would be fine, but what do you think?"

My father stopped darting daggers at me in the rearview mirror and drove off. He sighed. "Yes, that would be fine as long as the place is not one of those cheap resorts with naked dancing entertainers." Fully distracted from me now, he had moved on to controlling Adam's wedding. "And try to talk her out of a slutty wedding dress. I hate those new ones these girls wear now, showing off their cleavage everywhere. Keep it classy."

I thought about what kind of girl I'd take down the aisle if I were ever stupid enough to marry: *one slutty, stripper bride coming right up.*

DaddyJ007: How's my angel doing today?

L'Sucre22: I'm good, daddy. How are you?

I was chatting online with my latest sugar daddy. It was my junior year in university. I was majoring in business with a focus on public relations.

Whenever I had sex with a man, I became way too involved emotionally, even if he was a terrible lay. Well, let's face it, I hadn't had a good lay in forever or maybe ever. Most men's penises were too small compared to my purple dildo. Why did I spend so much time internet stalking some small dick man after fucking him once? I didn't know why, but I knew it wasn't healthy.

41

My brain seemed wired to go for guys who were not right for me: the one who ended up having a fiancé, the one who kept repeating "rape me" when I was on top, the one who stole my car and crashed it, the one who asked if I'd have sex with him and his sister at the same time...

Yet, I felt like I had some weird connection to each of these men after sex and thought we were in a relationship or that they would come back to be with me when everything in my head was screaming, "You don't even like him!" So, I was trying to cut myself off. Gain some perspective.

To avoid falling for the wrong guy again, I'd resorted to becoming a sugar baby online. No, I didn't need the money. I enjoyed the attention. The most exciting part was seeing how far I could push these daddies to give me extravagant gifts. It was a fun game; I didn't have to put out since I hadn't and wouldn't meet any of the men in person. I could flirt, control when and how long we would talk, and I could get myself off with my purple dildo. It was a win-win-win, in my opinion.

> DaddyJ007: Are you staying pure for me?

> L'Sucre22: Of course, daddy, always.

I was chatting with John, my daddy, who had

recently become my sole sugar daddy. *DaddyJ007* was one of my main tippers when I did camgirl shows; he'd never say anything, only give large tips. After a few weeks, John requested multiple private chats.

Over the past week, he asked if I would stop giving shows to anyone else so he could be my exclusive daddy. I agreed, and he sent me a monthly payment that was more than what all the other tippers had given me combined. John wanted me to roleplay as his pure young girlfriend, but he must have known I wasn't a virgin.

Always respectful and kind, he would ask about my days and how my classes were; he seemed genuinely interested in me as a person. I didn't reveal much; he thought I was using the money for university, and I let him think so.

I assumed he was a lonely old man with too much money and no family. Pretty sure he wanted a daughter. He bought me a Porsche over the summer, which I had painted in my favorite color, neon green. I took pictures in a schoolgirl outfit sitting in the front seat after I drove it the first time, then sent him the photos.

> DaddyJ007: Will you show me your pretty panties today?

I turned on my camera. John and I always chatted when I was in my apartment bedroom. I shared it with three roommates, including my friend Marissa. I often turned on a fan so they wouldn't hear what I was doing in my room, or I hoped they wouldn't.

"Sure, daddy." Kneeling on my bed in front of my laptop camera, I slowly started to lift the plaid skirt I was wearing to show off my white lacy thong. "I think you bought this for me."

"Angel, you look so pretty in it. You make your daddy hard just taking a peek at you." He had changed to voice chat but did not share a video.

"I wish I could see." John never turned on his camera if he had one. That was fine. I assumed he was fat and bald or had a micro-penis, maybe ashamed of his appearance. I was going to shower him with compliments no matter what.

"Would you like to?"

"Wow, yes. I've been imagining what you look like forever. I'd love to see my daddy's cock."

"Careful, angel. I don't want to hear that kind of filth from my little girl's mouth."

I pouted at the camera and started to pull down my skirt.

"But, since you've been such a good girl this past week, staying away from those university boys and your dildo, I'll reward you." John insisted I avoided sex with anyone else. He did not like me using any dildos or things that could "stretch" my vagina before he could. I used my dildo when he didn't know and would tell him I hadn't. He wanted to watch me move around or show off my underwear—

innocent stuff so far. I would stop it if I felt uncomfortable.

A video feed came up on our chat program. It showed a large, thick cock pulled out of some unzipped dress pants. John had defined abdominal muscles exposed by an opened dress shirt and a well-defined chest with some brown and gray hair. I was not expecting an attractive older man. I couldn't see his face.

"Oh, wow, daddy... I didn't expect such a big, thick cock."

John began to fondle himself. "Why don't you lower those panties and use one finger to touch yourself on your clit? You'll make daddy very happy."

I laid back with my head propped up on pillows, the camera between my legs. I had done this in private shows for others, but never for John. I slid my panties off and did as he asked. Only one finger to my clit, and I rubbed gently. I whimpered and watched John jerk his chubby penis harder.

I started to add a second finger, but John stopped. "No, angel. That's too much. You need to stay pure. Just one little finger. You must wait for your daddy's thick cock to enter you before you can get too much."

I thought I might die. It wasn't enough pressure or fullness. I was getting hot and couldn't go further. All I could think of was my purple dildo waiting in my nightstand drawer. I writhed my hips up to try to see if that would help.

"You need to learn to use only one finger, sweetheart... Daddy is the only one who can fulfill your needs."

Watching him stroke himself while using one finger was making me drenched. Squirming and moaning, I was hoping he'd give in to let me at least put it inside myself.

"I want to see my little girl's nipples. Can you take your top off? Then spread yourself open with two fingers so I can see how pure you are and pinch your little nipple. Can you do that for daddy?"

I did as he requested. Pulling off my T-shirt and unfastening my front-close bra, my large breasts popped out. I spread my legs and rolled my nipples while moaning for him in the camera. He groaned and yanked himself more vigorously.

"Spread your pussy, baby girl. Spread it with two fingers so I can see where I will come."

I laid back again, grasping one nipple and pinching it while spreading my cunt with two fingers.

"Oh, my little girl. I see how pure your tiny pussy is. So pink and pretty." His tight grip and rough pumps made it look like he was about to come.

"Daddy, can I please put a finger inside my pussy?"

"Mmm, angel. Yes, but only if you imagine this big cock inside you."

I put my finger inside, letting the heel of my hand rub my clit. I began to hump my hand with vigor.

"Oh, you look so tight. I think my cock may hurt you. Are you imagining me inside of you, baby girl?"

"Y-yes, daddy!" And looking at his dick, I was. I would come knowing I was getting this man off and feeling so sexy doing it.

John groaned and stroked himself until cum started spewing from his tip, all over his hand. He said, "Oh, I can't wait to pump this cum inside my little girl's pussy." I came thinking about having his cum inside of me.

It was for the best that I didn't know much about him. I couldn't stalk his social media, or I may have started to plan our wedding.

John used tissues and cleaned himself up. I pulled my skirt down. John put himself away and zipped up his pants. He turned off his camera but left his voice on.

John spoke as if we had just signed online, "Hello, angel."

"Your dick is so nice!" And I didn't have to bullshit.

John laughed. "Well, it would have to be to earn someone as beautiful as you." I blushed. I was blushing. This wasn't good. I was supposed to do this to set some distance. Now, I was blushing and wondering what John's favorite cake flavor was. "You make this old man so horny; I had to get that out of the way, precious. I'm sorry. You do mean more to me than sex. I enjoy your company. Now, truly, how was your day?"

John and I ended up chatting for another ten minutes before I needed to study. He didn't want me to know much about him, which was good for me, especially since I had seen his penis and he gave me an orgasm. Maybe he had an ugly face or was horribly disfigured. I wondered if he was married and had children. I didn't notice a wedding band.

We said goodnight. As soon as I shut off the chat app, I pulled out my purple dildo and got myself off again, thinking of what we had done.

Afterward, I decided I wasn't in the mood for studying and would head to the Ginger Lizard Lounge, a frequent hangout for university students. I knocked on Marissa's door, but she refused to go. Sharice, another roommate, must have been out practicing her violin. Kinsley walked in from the grocery, bags of food covering her arms. I quickly helped her unload. "You want to head to the Lounge with me?"

"When?"

"Right now," I told her, putting away the oatmeal in a cabinet.

"Uh... sure! Why not? Semester just started, and I don't have much going on yet." Kinsley and I became friends through Marissa. She and Marissa had been roomies their freshman year. Last year, when we all got this four-bedroom together, I got to know her and Sharice more. Kinsley was usually down for a good night on the town, but only if it didn't interfere with her classes. She was pre-med like my older sister Emilia had been. Emilia was now in medical school.

Kinsley and I walked the mile and a half to the town's center. Other than the university, there wasn't much to see. We had a couple of restaurants and a few bars. There was one dance club. Usually, all the students went to a certain spot on different nights: Sundays were pizza night at Tony's, Taco Tuesdays at Manny's, Thursdays were at Lizard Lounge, and Fridays or Saturdays were either a fraternity or sorority party or the warehouse dance club on the edge of the downtown area.

When we arrived, the Lounge was packed with students. Being the first week, no one had much to do other than party and meet up with returning friends. I was wearing my little plaid skirt from earlier and a vintage band T-shirt. I paired it with some ankle boots and a hobo bag. Kinsley nudged me and pointed to the bar. It was too loud to hear each other, with live music coming from the stage area.

We weaseled through the crowd and ordered our drinks. I was waiting to pay when the bartender shook his head and pointed to a group of guys at the end of the bar. One of the guys nodded at me and held up his drink. I smiled and nodded in return. I recognized the group as part of Theta Rho Zeta, the rich boy fraternity that held the infamous Red Night parties throughout the year. Red Night was basically an exclusive orgy where playboys got off on having the hottest men and women at their disposal for a night.

Xavier Cardell was president of TRZ this year, which probably meant Levi Joseph was an officer. I had avoided Cardell and Joseph on campus as much as possible over the last two years, only seeing them in the business building a few times before I would turn around and walk the other way. During sophomore year, I had an economics class with Levi, but I sat in the very back of the large auditorium, so I don't think he noticed.

The man who bought me a drink started to walk over. He was tall and broad-shouldered, with blond hair fluffed up on top of his head. A scruffy beard covered his square jaw. As he approached, he smiled warmly. He leaned over so he could speak into my ear. It was difficult to hear.

"Hey, I'm Carter." He held out his hand for me to shake.

"Hi." I took his hand. "Elle."

"Elle? You're the most beautiful woman I have seen in a long time. Just wanted to get to know you a little better." That was nice, and he wasn't staring at my chest.

"Thanks. You in TRZ?"

"Yeah. Hey, can we talk on the patio? Too loud here." Carter nodded his head towards the back door leading to the patio. It was a pleasant night, so I tapped Kinsley on the shoulder and pointed to the door. She nodded, but was talking with some other guy.

Carter held the door for me as we stepped out of the loud music, and my ears felt full of hot air for a moment as I adjusted to the different pressure. The moon was out, casting a glow on the outdoor area covered in twinkling yellow lights. Small iron tables with chairs lined the edges, while larger wooden picnic tables filled the center. There were a lot of students out enjoying drinks and conversations.

"Want to sit?" Carter found us an empty table with two chairs. "Sorry, I was having a hard time hearing you inside. Yes, I'm in TRZ. I'm an officer. Senior. How about you?"

"Well, I'm not in TRZ and not an officer." Carter chuckled. "I am a junior, though. Business."

"Architecture." He pointed to himself, smiled, and said, "I hope you're single."

I laughed. "I am. How about you?"

"Yes, very much so. Hoping to change that, though." His eyes sparkled at me. This flirting part was so fun. Carter was kind, attractive, and interested. It had been a while since I had done this in person and not online.

"Oh? How were you going to change that?"

"Well, I guess first by inviting you to the Red Night formally, hoping you'd show up for me. You ever been?"

I cringed. So he wanted to bang at the sex party.

Here I was, hoping someone would take me on an actual date. "Uh, no. Never been. Heard they get wild, though."

"Oh, I didn't mean... I'm sorry. I wasn't just inviting you for, well, you know. I wanted to hang out with you more. Thought the invitation would earn me some cool points." He smiled.

"It does. I'd love to go to hang out. I mean, I don't know what will happen, but it would be nice to see what the party is like." I felt like I may be in trouble with Carter. If he made me orgasm, I might have to change my name. "What's your last name?"

"Cline. You gonna stalk me online now?" He laughed at his own joke. I probably was.

"Mine's Townsend."

"Well, Elle Townsend. Let me get a picture with you for my 'gram, then. That way, you'll be the most beautiful woman on my feed when you stalk it." He stood up near the fence of the patio and motioned for me to join under his arm. I got up, and he started to take a picture with me, but he ended up kissing my cheek as he did so. That was cute; he was cute.

"Hey, now. Don't get too fresh," I said, but I giggled. He looked into my eyes and kissed me gently on the lips.

"I needed that to tide me over until I can see you again. Can I get your number?" We exchanged digits, and I finished my drink. Carter bought me another. We chatted a bit about the football team's chances this year, freshman classes we may have had in common, and whatever band was playing on stage. He went inside and returned to hand me a formal Red Night invitation in a fancy envelope. We said goodnight, and he hugged me.

Maybe things weren't as hopeless in the romance department as I thought.

"Hell, yeah, brothers. Picked up a dirty slut for the party. Heard she let Cody Meyer ass fuck her on top of their keg at the Delta party." Carter Cline was running his mouth again. The kid was annoying. Always pretending to brag over some woman when I knew very well he was fucking my brother's fiancé.

Oh, yeah. I'd seen him and Whitney at last year's Red Night and then again on Halloween. And once on a Sunday at the university library.

When I tried to tell Adam, I was "being dramatic" or "misinterpreted" what I saw, then it was "I'll handle it." He argued with her once, but then they made up. She probably told him some lies and gave him a blowie, and things were back on.

You would think Adam would have a clue when Whitney postponed their wedding six times because things weren't "perfect." I was hoping it got rescheduled until I could show him some video footage of the cheating cunt. Women were all the same.

"Joseph, check it out." Carter brought his phone over to me to show me a picture. *No fucking way.*

"Elle Townsend?" I asked.

"Yeah, man. You know her?" Carter looked a bit worried. "You ever fuck her before?"

"Yeah, I know her." *Damn it.* I couldn't think of anything quick enough to turn him off her. Telling him she's a whore wouldn't work; he'd get turned on more. "Just be careful, man. I think that girl is looking to get knocked up as soon as she can."

Carter frowned. *Yes! Got him.* "Oh. You think so? She's looking to settle down?"

"Pretty sure that girl is in college for her M.R.S. degree, if you know what I mean," I lied.

"Really? I thought she was the one on the keg at the Delta party—" Carter questioned.

Xavier loped into the meeting room, where we were getting ready to start. "No, that wasn't her. It was Caitlyn Watson." We all laughed.

"Yeah, I saw her!" A few of the brothers chuckled and yelled out in agreement.

"What'd you do to her this time, Cardell," Carter asked.

Xavier sighed and shook his head with exasperation. It was probably the same tired situation it always was. Caitlyn Watson had been obsessed with Xavier for years. They had hooked up on occasion, but whenever Xavier would bang someone else or pay attention to another girl, she'd try her best to make him jealous. Guess she thought letting the president of Delta fuck her in the ass on top of the keg would do it. The problem for her was that Xavier didn't give a shit about her.

Mr. President Xavier Cardell ran the meeting smoothly, as usual. Theta Rho Zeta was prepping for our quarterly Red Night in a couple of weeks. Someone from student health spoke about lining us up to get tested for sexually transmitted diseases beforehand. With the amount of money that Cardell Enterprises donated to the university, we would be gifted supplies (a truckful of condoms and lube, mainly).

I stepped up to the podium to share my piece as treasurer, explaining how much was allocated for the event (No, Tyson, we didn't have a budget for cocaine this year; bring your own). Security stood up to explain the check-in procedure for guests. They would be checking identification and invitations.

Lawyers for our fraternity, paid for by Cardell and someone's attorney daddy, spoke about the legal ramifications of any problems that may arise. All attendees knew that by coming, they were legally bound to discretion and consenting to sex while at the party. It was the same as all the previous years for the last few decades.

When I sat back down, my thoughts turned back to Elle and the Red Night party. It was burning me up inside that Carter had asked her. I should probably keep an eye on her if she was going to hang out with him, maybe lure her away and stay sober enough that I could actually fuck her. Just once. Something in the back of my brain told me it wasn't a good idea for me to have sex with Elle, though.

I didn't have anyone I was thinking of bringing. Most of the attractive women on campus had ridden my dick before. I was running out of options, especially since I'd also gone through their sisters or mothers, as well. It was becoming a hassle to ensure my "one and done" policy was in effect. Not that I usually wanted another go around, but the rule had to be bent if I was ever going to get laid again.

FATHER

Come home as soon as your meeting is finished.

Shit. I swore internally, sitting in my chair at the meeting when I got the text from my father. Warren had been on my case more since he found out about me fucking Samantha a few weeks prior. She must have told him about us; I would never. Father yelled at me about not having anyone to take to the Cardell's summer party because I had screwed all his dates (it was true).

Amid that argument, I yelled, "She's not my

mom!" Then I laughed hysterically. So he threatened to cut me off again, and I pretended to behave for a month. Rinse and repeat.

I had to break it off with his women to keep him off my back, which limited my options for fucks further. Surprisingly, Samantha wasn't too pleased, but I did what I had to do. She took it harder than I thought she would, even crying, until I awkwardly slipped out of her house while she was dressed in lingerie.

Cue this month's argument; it was overdue. I wondered what it would be about.

I parked my Mercedes at my father's house, and my heart sank when I saw Adam's car. This meant an ambush of some sort. Maybe it had to do with me trying to tell him about Whitney's cheating. Perhaps they wanted me to keep quiet about it. I'd lie in wait until I could get the proof I needed and capture it on video sometime.

I entered the house and called out, but there was no answer. The staff would have left for the day; it was late. I found my father, brother... and Whitney in my father's office. Flopping down on the couch at the back of the room, I waited for the flogging to begin. They all were quiet, as if expecting me to greet them.

Eventually, my father spoke. "Son, Adam and Whitney have an announcement."

Adam cleared his throat and turned to me behind him. "Whitney and I are getting married in six weeks in the Bahamas. It will be at the first resort we picked out." Adam was trying hard not to look at Whitney. Whitney was still turned around and not looking at me.

I snorted. "Okay."

"Do you have something you'd like to say?" My father was baiting me.

"No." I paused. "You're getting married in six weeks at the same resort you picked out *two years ago* when you first decided to do this." I chortled. "I mean, I'll believe it when I see it."

My father sighed. Adam said gently, "There is no going back on this one." He looked solemnly at Whitney finally as he said, "This is the last time we change our plans. We've already paid for the wedding. Of course," he narrowed his eyes at Whitney carefully here, "since it is so soon, not all the guests can make it, but we wanted to let you know so you can miss some classes. I have to have my best man there."

"He'll be there, Adam." My father spoke for me.

"Of course, I'll be there." Time away from school to party on a beach for a weekend? Sign me up. I wondered if Elle would be there. "Who's all going?"

"Whitney's family and her maid of honor, Emilia, Emilia's boyfriend, Jake, Elizabeth, and her husband. Of course, you and Dad..." Adam listed off a couple of his friends. "Oh, and Elle, I think, is going, too, but she doesn't have a date. I think you'll escort her in the process?" He looked at Whitney, who shook her head.

"Elle will be lined up with Tim," Whitney said.

My heart skipped a beat at the mention of her name. "Sounds like fun."

My brother and his fiancé made some excuses and said their goodbyes, and I was about to do the same, annoyed that I had driven all the way over to this mirage of a home, when my father stopped me.

"Levi, wait. I'd like to speak with you. Please, sit." He pointed to the chair Adam had vacated. My father waited until his firstborn left the room and shut the door before continuing. "I keep hearing reports that you are still engaging in illicit affairs with women around town."

"No, I made it through all your dates. I don't have anyone left to screw."

"Levi, please." He pointed his fingers underneath his nose. "Please, son, tell me you use protection. We cannot have an illegitimate child coming to steal my money." And there it was.

"I mean, I try to pull out most of the time, but it feels so good. It's really hard, you know?" The veins on the sides of his head were twitching. "I'll stick it in their asses next time. I'm sorry. Ass sex is responsible sex."

"That is enough." My father stood up. "I was probably way too lax with you as I had been with Adam, but you are different." He began pacing. "I don't want to hear any more of your dallies. You are not to engage in any philandering activities any longer."

"Geez, Mr. Cleaver. May I court a pretty girl if I meet one?"

"I'm serious, Levi. I can't have you screwing your way into a bastard child or hurting the wrong girl. You know what things are like now. Any of these girls could say anything—the shame they'd bring upon our family. You could be in jail. How sure are you that you don't already have a...?"

I huffed. "No, Father. I have not knocked up anyone. I always wear a condom. Do you want me to get sterilized? Would that make you happy?" Maybe I should do it. Maybe that would make him proud of me for once. Hello, this is Levi, my son that didn't marry a cheating whore and produce a bunch of bastards.

"Heavens, no. I want you to be more like your brother. Settling down, dating someone regularly. Someone *respectable*. Getting ready for marriage. You're a senior in college now. Most boys are thinking about those things."

"Like Adam..."

"Yes, like Adam." My father sat, thinking he had won me over.

"So, like with a cheating whore for a fiancé? Is that what I'm to expect?"

"Watch your mouth. For that, I may call Frederick tomorrow and have you disowned."

I was always on the edge of screaming, "Do it already!" Just so my misery of living under his iron rule could end. I held my tongue; I knew when he was serious, and I wasn't quite ready to cut the noose yet. Probably after graduation, when I could approach Mr. Townsend. My crypto portfolio was doing great, but stocks and funds were not.

"Okay, Father. I will keep it in my pants." Fat chance. I would be more discreet. Whom did I know that could keep it on the down-low?

"And there will be no more Red Nights," he commanded.

"Uh... what?"

"I said, no Red Nights. Those parties are disgusting displays of debauchery. I don't want someone filming you or forgetting their birth control." He gave me the look again that he was planning to end my life if I said anything other than yes.

"Yes, sir."

"So you are to come here the night of the event and spend the night."

I laughed. "You're serious? I'm an adult."

"*Are* you?"

"Father, I am twenty-two years old. You want me to stay here the night of Red Night?"

"Yes. Do we have a problem?"

"No, sir."

After I was "dismissed," I drove as fast as I could to the liquor store before they closed. I grabbed my favorite bottle of bourbon and went to the house.

Jackson, Chris, and a couple of other guys were in the kitchen for a late-night snack.

To get the room's attention, I yelled, "Who's ready to fucking *party*?"

"I'm out. Got a morning class." Chris dipped.

"I'm in! Let's go." Jackson was always down for fun. A few of the guys agreed, and we started taking shots. We moved to the games room and played some beer pong. Smoked some weed. I convinced one of the pledges to tap a keg, and we did some keg stands. Lost at beer pong. Twice. Smoked someone's bong. Snorted some cocaine. Maybe some more cocaine.

Made it to the hot tub. Decided to call someone, maybe Tiffany? Brooke? Kara? I wondered if Carter had Elle's number. Yeah... that was a fantastic fucking idea.

Made it to Carter's room. Nope, went to the bathroom on that floor and puked. Waited on the toilet for a bit, then stood up and weaved back to Carter's room. He was pissed that I woke him up. He held the door closed, so I couldn't open it when I tried. I didn't need to see his dong, anyway; I needed some pussy.

"What time is it?" I asked him after finishing the bourbon, standing there with the empty bottle. I tried to hand it to him through the half open door, but he wouldn't take it.

"It's three a.m., you fuck."

"I just need Elle Townsend's number. E-l-l-l-l-e," I

said it slowly so he would understand me. My tongue felt so fat in my mouth, which was dry as sandpaper.

"I'll give it to you tomorrow. Go to bed, Joseph. You're wasted."

"No, no, no, no," I tried to push open his door, but he stopped me again.

"Fine, wait a sec." He went inside, and I saw a woman lying in his bed. Was that... It looked like Whitney. I couldn't find my phone to take a picture. Fuck, where was it? Where was my fucking phone? Quick! Carter grabbed his phone from his dresser and brought it back to me, but it was locked.

"Open. Open. Open," I said impatiently. My dick was rock hard. I couldn't lose this erection. He unlocked his phone while I was still telling him to open it. He found the number and texted it to me. Oh, I realized my phone was in my back pocket as it vibrated. Thought I had checked there.

"Shanks you..."

Carter slammed his door in my face.

Somehow I made it to my bedroom. I had enough control to type out what I wanted to say. I needed to make sure it was perfect. Surely she would come over if I said it right.

> L. i love u. i always ahve. i need u pls come over.

> COME get it?

I sent them. I was betting she would come over. I needed to stay awake so that I could be with her. She could be the girl, the one my father talked about. She could be it.

> im serious plse i want to get married for real this time

> ur so ducking hot

> just once come over serious need that hotness on em

I don't remember the rest of the night.

I t was Red Night, and I was picking out my outfit. From what I knew of the event, people dressed up in either dresses or completely bare. A mask was suggested to maintain anonymity, but I didn't care about that. Elle Townsend was expected to be at TRZ functions; it's what I was known for.

I chose a nude-lined, sparkly mini dress. It had a deep-V neck all the way down to my belly button, showcasing the diamonds pierced within. My hair was tied into a high ponytail, and my ears dripped with clear jewels. My sexy clear lace-up high heels made me taller than I already was, but Carter was tall, so kissing him wouldn't be strange.

Carter texted me a few times over the last few weeks but was too busy with his architecture projects to hang out. It would be the first time I had seen him since Lizard Lounge. My plan of attack would be to avoid having sex with him. He was very attractive and kind and said he wanted to get to know me better. I would hold on to that. *Please don't give in unless he asks you on a date*, was what I told myself. If he made me orgasm, I'd be done for. Elle Cline had a nice ring to it. I'd already stalked his social media every day since I met him.

I knew from previous parties at the Theta Rho Zeta house that they had a tranquil pool and steamy hot tub. In my Birkin bag, I packed some flip-flops and a bikini with a sexy coverup dress in case I decided to hang out there. The weather was warm for September; if I were outside, I'd be less likely to have sex with Carter in a bedroom. *Don't do it until a date.*

John and I were on a three-day-per-week schedule of masturbating on camera together. He still thought of me as a pure girl, and I didn't want to upset him by telling him any details of my extracurricular activities. I certainly hadn't mentioned anything to him about Carter. Or Red Night. Or about the weird drunk texts I had to block.

I thought perhaps the texts were sent to the wrong number. But the person said "hotness," and I only knew one person who said that. Levi didn't have my number, and I wasn't sure why he would want it other than to torture me. The texts had come at 3 a.m., so it was likely him.

After arriving at the TRZ manor (yes, a full stone castle with stables, guest cottages, and gargoyles), I tossed the keys to my neon green Porsche at the valets. They were impressed with my car. The security guard at the front door searched my bag and my tits, but let me go. Guests were not allowed phones, but I had left mine at the apartment.

The first floor of the manor was packed with college students, and I had a hard time finding Carter. Trying to be sly, wanting to avoid being seen by Xavier and Levi, I stuck to the walls and slinked around corners. My glittery low-cut dress was making waves, though, and people noticed me. Several people were chatting and flirting at the bar in the reception area. Most women were dressed like me, but others wore lingerie or costumes. Some of the men were buck-naked, and some were in tuxedos.

DJ music flooded the hall outside the big party room as I slipped inside. The dance floor held a few stripper poles with some women writhing on them gracefully. I stood and watched, swaying in the misty red lights of the room. A man put his arms around my waist and whispered in my ear, "Mmm, wanna go upstairs?" I could feel his mediocre erection between my ass cheeks.

I squirmed away. "No, thank you."

Continuing my hunt downstairs, I recognized several people from parties on campus. Fortunately, I did not see any signs of my childhood bullies. I heard Xavier liked to host a private party in his bedroom and briefly wondered if Levi was in there... and who he was with. A few guys I knew grabbed me or tried to kiss me, but I easily shook them off with a flirty laugh. I needed a drink.

As I headed toward the dining room, Carter walked out of the kitchen and saw me. He was wearing a black button-down shirt over khaki shorts with leather sandals. He smiled brightly and said, "*Damn*, sexy."

"Hey, you look sexy yourself."

He leaned over to kiss my cheek. I could smell cinnamon and alcohol on his breath. "Need a drink?"

"Yes, please."

Carter pulled me by the hand to the bar in the reception area. A bartender mixed my Tom Collins while Carter stared at my chest. The dress was advertising all my goods; I couldn't fault him for looking. Downing my first drink, I started to request a second, but Carter interrupted.

"Do you want to head upstairs? I could show you my room."

"Can we just hang for a bit first?" So, he *did* invite me to fuck me. I should have known.

Carter put his hand around my waist and gently laid it on my lower back. "Do you want to go outside? It's pretty nice out tonight."

"Yes, that sounds amazing." We started back towards the entryway to the open patio doors. "Is there a place I could change into my bikini?"

"Yep. We have a pool house over there. I'll meet you back out here with another drink." Carter smiled.

A little white wood-clad cottage stood near the sparkling pool, and I went inside. It was a beautiful guest house complete with a kitchenette and bathroom. I dressed in the bedroom. As I was finishing up and tying my white triangle top, James Stevenson and Jackson Riley waltzed in naked, grasping at one another's bodies in the throes of passion. They didn't even see me as I brushed past them quickly on my way out.

James was Marissa's boyfriend... But Marissa and James had some sort of sex agreement. The legal jargon of the invite bound me not to discuss what I saw here. I would have to ask her about it artfully after the party. I wasn't sure if she knew about James and Jackson being alone together. Where was she? Was she here?

Returning to the pool area, I stowed my bag in an outdoor cabinet under some cushions and made my way to a swim trunk clad Carter in my little white bikini. I knew my overindulgent breasts were about to pop out of the top, and the G-string I wore didn't hide much in the back.

Carter's eyes bulged as he saw me and handed me a second cocktail. "Holy shit. I thought the dress would do me in, but this..." He grabbed his crotch without a hint of subtlety. His erection was outlined clearly in his shorts. "I would suggest the hot tub, but it's occupied. Unless you want to try to join in."

I glanced over to see Chloe, a woman I'd hung out with at several happenings. She was dishing out blowjobs to several men who stood in a circle in the hot tub. She would hold two cocks and bob her head on one before switching to the other. Then she would turn and grab two more dicks and continue around the circle. Each man was jerking off near her face when they weren't being sucked off. Occasionally one would orgasm, grab her head and shove in so she could swallow.

"Maybe in a bit," I said, raising my glass. I downed it. This party was already lit, and I needed a third drink. A waiter brought over another cocktail as soon as I finished my glass. Carter grabbed my hand and led me to the pool. We sat on the edge, legs in the warmed water, looking out onto the glistening surface lit with red lights.

Several people were in the pool making out or having sex. One couple was next to us. The man thrust slowly into the woman against the side while they were in the water. She was moaning softly while he pumped into her.

A foursome of people had taken up residence on the diving board near the pool's deep end. A petite brunette woman was laid out on the board while Chris (I recognized him) was fucking her pussy and sucking a standing man's cock. The upright man was straddling the brunette woman. Serene, a girl from my marketing class, came over to the group and knelt next to the brunette woman; she began sucking on the woman's nipples while fingering herself.

I noticed two women on a lounge chair across the pool from us. One was snacking on the other's pussy while several men stood around to watch. Some held their dicks out, masturbating over the women's writhing bodies. One man seemed to be vocally instructing them on what to do. "That's it, now suck her little clit, baby. I knew my girlfriend would love pussy. You love this, right? You love to eat pussy?" The girl eating looked up at him and nodded. He spanked her ass in encouragement. That caused one of the other men to spurt his load all over the breasts of the woman being eaten, who then clenched her thighs and screamed in ecstasy.

As I was taking in my surroundings and sipping my lemony drink, Carter slowly massaged my back. He laid light kisses on my shoulder as he sat next to me. He caught my chin with a finger and leaned in to kiss me. So much for just wanting to hang out.

"Fuck, you're so sexy," he whispered in my mouth. Carter must have been taking shots before I got there; he tasted of strong liquor.

I kissed him, but pulled back to slow things down. As I did, Levi Joseph strolled into the pool area and sat down *directly across from us* on the edge of the pool. Short swim trunks framed his body, a magnificent work of art.

Even though we went to different private schools for high school, I knew he swam competitively (I stalked him online). He still had a fantastic swimmer's body, except now it was a man's and not a boy's. He leaned back on veiny forearms, showcasing his cut abs with a deep V leading to something large poking beneath his shorts.

"Don't mind me," he said, gazing directly at us.

Carter and I were annoyed, but as I started to say something snippy to Levi about his audacity, Carter cupped my head and tilted it so that he could suck behind my ear and down my neck. I gasped and watched Levi's eyes narrow and his jaw clench. Oh, this was working better than anything I could say to him...

Carter's mouth made its way to my collarbone. He gently put a hand on my stomach and then slid it to my thigh. Levi's eyes continued to fill with rage, watching us. He leaned forward as if he were about to say something, his tight pectoral muscles flexing as he did so.

Two tall blonde women approached him; both were naked and had model bodies. One sat beside him, almost on his lap, and the other got into the water between his legs. Levi glanced to see who they were, then smirked at me. He wrapped his arm around the one next to him and kissed her neck with a wide open mouth. The one in the water started to nuzzle his crotch with her entire face.

Not sure why, he wasn't mine by any stretch, but I was filled with jealousy. How dare he? I turned my head to Carter and began to suck his neck back. I let his hand drift up and cup my pussy, humping his palm slightly when he did. As nonchalantly as possible, I let my head fall back to glance at Levi.

Levi was staring at my face intently. His expression was heated with lust and anger, golden brown eyes glaring at me. The girl between his legs had lowered his shorts and pulled out his beautiful, thick cock, and was starting to lick it. I couldn't make it out fully, but I could tell it was large.

The girl beside him stopped kissing his neck to slide lithely into the water next to the other woman. He glanced down at the two between his widened legs. Levi caressed their heads as they started to blow him together. The first one would suck for a while, then the other. Levi's head fell backward with pleasure. When he brought it up again, he looked right at me.

Carter had slipped his fingers inside my bikini bottoms and rubbed my clit. He added a second finger and began diving his fingers inside me. I turned my body so he could hold me closer, my head resting on his shoulder. Carter took one of my hands and put it on his crotch. I could feel a small, erect penis in his shorts. Ugh, of course, he had a small dick. Subtly, I moved my eyes to watch Levi and his huge cock. I felt him staring at me.

The two women were sharing Levi, swallowing him together. One would bob on his cock head while the other sucked his shaft sideways or suck his balls while gazing up at him. He continued to run his fingers through their hair, but his eyes were focused like lasers on mine.

I felt myself going over the edge as Carter fingered me, but I didn't want to orgasm. I just met Carter and knew if I did come, I'd end up hurting myself again. I needed to slow things down; this wasn't part of the plan. Not only that, but I knew I was using Carter to make Levi jealous.

It was backfiring; I wanted to be one of the women between Levi's legs. I wanted to be sucking his cock, feeling him come down my throat. I wanted Levi's fingers inside me, his kisses on my neck. My crush had never ended, and I hated myself for that.

Tugging on Carter's arm, I tried to squirm away so he would stop. "Stop, please," I whispered to him. He didn't stop. "Carter, stop," I said more insistently.

Carter lunged at me, forcing me back onto the rough concrete patio. He was on top of me in a flash, tongue down my throat and trying to pull his dick out of his shorts. I tried to move a knee between his legs and turn my head to say no, but he pressed his hips hard into me. The lower half of my body was trapped by his.

Suddenly, he was gone. My body was still lying on the concrete. Above me, I could see Levi strangling Carter with a lock around his neck while punching him repeatedly in the face. Carter was trying to flip Levi off of his body. They were grappling with each other, arms wrapped around each other's chests. A few men came over from their activities to try to break things up. One man grabbed Levi and pulled him back while someone else grabbed Carter. Levi tried to break away to hit Carter again. He yelled, "She said stop, motherfucker. That means you stop!"

I sat up and adjusted my suit. Carter spat blood from his mouth onto the concrete and wiped it with the back of his hand, checking for more. He shoved the guy holding him off and stalked towards the house, saying, "Not worth it."

Levi was still going to go after him as he thrashed against the two men that held him. "Calm the fuck down, Joseph. Calm down. Let it go," one of the guys was trying to tell him, but Levi wasn't going to let it go. His reddened face made that clear. I stood up and started to go to Levi when I spotted Marissa looking dazed in front of the pool house.

"Oh, my god. You were invited, too? And you showed up? I have so much to tell you." I was ready to spill all the drama, but the look on her face was clear. She must have seen her boyfriend and Jackson together. I needed to get her out of there.

I tiptoed to Levi, who was now being wrestled by

three men towards the grounds beyond the hedge fence. "Levi," I approached, but one of the men tried to stop me with a hand on my shoulder.

"Not now," said a huge guy (I think named George).

"Levi, thank you," I yelled at him, but I didn't think he heard me. The men were moving him into the lawn, and he was still struggling and roaring at them to let him go.

I watched him walk off on his own, then turned to collect my bag from the cabinet, threw on my coverup, and rushed my friend home.

four

LEVI

I was going to kill Carter Cline.

First off, I'd had to listen to him talk about Elle's body for the last month. I wanted to vomit every time he said "tits" and "ass," describing what he planned to do to each of them—licking his lips. He'd look right at me and smirk like he knew it was driving me mad.

Second, I blamed him for having to spend Red Night at my father's house. Don't ask for the logic explaining that one. Carter Cline was now my nemesis, so no explanation was needed. I was free to blame him for all my life's problems. Years from now, if I stubbed my toe, I would yell out in pain, "Fuck Carter!"

I was late to the party because I had to sneak out of my old room at Father's house. I'd gotten rusty from lack of practice since my high school days. Not caring if I got a speeding ticket, I drove as fast as possible, but was still too late to interrupt Carter from getting his paws on Elle.

Third, Carter tried to force himself on Elle. That was the most important point. This man deserved death by papercuts, and I was there to bring down the hammer of justice.

I was pacing in my swim trunks on the lawn. Big G stood ten feet away in case I tried to run again. He was huge, but slower than I was. I imagined cutting to his left, juking him to the right, then sprinting for the house. I was betting Carter was in his room by now.

Xavier started walking from the house to meet me. I didn't give a shit what he said; I was going through with my mission. I continued my animal stalk back and forth across a patch in the lawn.

Xavier stood like a statue before me, arms at his sides. "What happened?"

"Fucking Cline tried to force himself on Elle," I told him with a death glare. If he even tried to defend him...

"I already told him to pack up and leave. He's out. It was in front of enough witnesses. I'll talk with the dean next week. I'm sure his daddy will settle the case to avoid jail time."

"Oh... huh. Well, good." I felt a little better. Xavier always knew what to do. Big G eyed me from five feet away.

Xavier spoke, "Yeah, so I think the more important thing is... how is Elle? She okay?"

"I don't know. I think she left." I paused for a moment. "Should I go check on her, you think?"

Xavier gave me this look like I had missed an entirely obvious point.

"Right, I should go check on her." I nodded mainly to myself to psych myself up. Just thinking about seeing her alone, talking to her one on one... I got nervous.

I passed the pool area, with Xavier and Big G walking behind me. I knew they would keep an eye on me until Carter was out of the house, ensuring I didn't do anything crazy. Kara and Brooke were still in the pool area, discussing what had happened with curious partiers.

"Sorry, ladies. I need to take off. Thanks for the good time." I smiled at them. They were always down to get down, so I was sure they'd find more partners for the evening if they hadn't already done so. I had enjoyed the look on Elle's face as they sucked me off. As much as I hated watching her with Carter, it felt good to know she was as jealous as I was.

After a quick shower and change in my room, I headed to her apartment complex. Xavier knew the address. It was almost two in the morning, well past visiting hours for the girls' dormitory, even though she lived in an upperclassman building. I knocked on the glass door, noticing that the woman with glasses at the front desk was one I had slept with a year ago or so. Maybe she'd take pity on me.

I kept tapping on the door when she finally lowered her phone to glance up at me. I used my smile. She got up and came to open the door slightly.

"Hey..." Fuck, what was her name? "Mary." She smiled. Yes, nailed it. "I know this is unusual, but there is a big emergency, and I need to get in touch with Elle Townsend. I have her phone number, but my phone is broken and not dialing out. Can you dial it for me?"

Mary eyed me suspiciously. "What kind of emergency?"

I made my face as solemn as possible. "There was an accident... I need to speak with her in person."

Poor Mary looked terrified. "Oh, okay, come in." She led me to her desk area, looked at the phone number, and then used the office phone to call Elle.

"Um, Levi Joseph is here to see you. He says there has been an emergency and needs to speak with you in person. Can I let him up?"

I thought this might be a bad idea. Maybe she was mad and going to say no. I heard her say thanks while I raged earlier tonight, so perhaps she would have mercy on me.

Mary hung up the phone. "She says you can go up. Apartment two twenty-one." I thanked her and started to walk away when she said, "Don't tell anyone

I let you." Flashing my dazzling smile, I told her it was our secret.

I darted towards the stairs, not wanting to waste time by taking the elevator. Elle wanted to see me. That was an excellent sign.

As I ran down the hall, I saw a door open midway, Elle's long, bare leg sticking out of it. "What are you doing here? It's two a.m.," she yelled in a whisper.

I almost spoke, but she shushed me with a finger to her plump lips and pointed at me to come inside. We went into the apartment, and I followed her to her room. If I thought the bikini would make me hard as nails, her little ruffly shirt and shorts set would cause me to come in my sweatpants if I felt a breeze on my dick.

When we reached her room, she stood on the far side and crossed her arms. This only pushed her double Ds up higher. "Well?"

"Are you okay?" I hadn't been alone with Elle since that day in eighth grade. My erection started to grow with tactile memory.

"I'm okay. Thank you, Levi. I don't know what would have happened if you hadn't been there. But you could have called or texted."

"Uh... I think you have my number blocked," I confessed.

She giggled, and her body relaxed. "Oh, that *was* you. How drunk were you?"

"One hundred and ten percent drunk. I aced the

drunk test and got extra credit." She laughed. I couldn't wait to hear it again. Moving closer to her, I placed a hand on her shoulder.

"Seriously, I came over to make sure you are okay." She moved into my arm, and something primal enveloped me. I needed to ensure she was protected in every way, to make sure she had everything she needed and didn't want for anything.

"Yeah, I'm okay." She turned to nuzzle my neck. Another flashback to the time we made out in Trent's bedroom. Mangoes. R&B music. I hugged her, but not as tightly as I wanted.

"Do you need to talk? Do you need food or some water, anything?"

She spoke into my neck and chest, "Can you just hold me for a while?"

Visions of fucking her into the mattress crossed my mind before I pushed it out for the better image of laying on the bed all night with this beautiful woman in my arms.

"Absolutely." My dick hardened, but I was mainly filled with awe that Elle Townsend had asked if I'd hold her. *Down, boy.*

She pulled me onto her bed, and I held her to my chest. Our bodies turned toward one another. She gathered up her comforter and pulled it over us, but I stopped her long enough to take off my shoes and socks. We settled, and I thought she'd fall asleep and wasn't sure what I would do then, maybe turn off her lamp and sneak out? If she did, should I stay? I wanted to stay but was unsure how she would feel in the morning.

"Do you remember sharing your Kit Kats with me in elementary school?" She kept her head in my chest.

"Ha! How could I forget? I loved Kit Kats. But your face would get so bright when I'd give you a piece. I couldn't help myself. Xavier always got mad that I didn't share with him."

She looked at me. "You didn't share with Xavier?"

"No. Stingy bastard never gave me any of his Oreos."

"I never gave you anything."

"You gave me my first kiss."

"I thought that was just a bet." She looked down again, hiding her face.

"Well, technically, you gave me my first *and* second kisses, then."

"You were counting—"

"Our wedding? Yeah. That was my first kiss."

She laughed. "So when you drunk texted me about getting married—"

"I don't remember what I said. I'm sorry about that." That was a lie. I still had the texts. I only wished she didn't remember.

"Don't be. It was funny."

I paused. I had to tell her. I couldn't keep it in any longer. I swallowed hard. "Elle, I took the bet at

Trent's, but I did it because I wanted you. I've had a crush on you forever."

"Really?" Her big light green eyes peered into my soul. I nodded because I couldn't speak. "But you called me Smelly Ellie for *years*. You laughed at me after that bet." She started to move away from me, but I grabbed her tightly.

"I was a kid. I was mean 'cause I liked you."

"That's stupid." She snuggled into me again.

"I accept that." I ran my fingers through her white-blond hair and tried not to think about the overwhelming urge to kiss her and taste her fruity breath again. "You going to the Bahamas in a couple of weeks?"

"Yeah. I am not looking forward to it."

"Why's that?"

She sighed. "It's time I'll have to spend around my mother and sisters. It's worse right now because I'm not dating anyone, so they'll spend their time trying to set me up with a Kennedy cousin or a pre-med."

"You, too, huh?"

She wrinkled her brow. "Your parents trying to set you up with a Kennedy or a pre-med?"

I chuckled, "No, it's just my father. My mother hasn't been around in years. I forgot you hadn't met him. It's better you haven't. He wants me to settle down like Adam."

"That's stupid. Whitney is cheating on him with some TRZ guy."

I about fell off the bed. "You knew about that?"

"Yeah. Figured it out and then saw her making out with someone in a bar a while ago."

"It was Carter."

"What? Carter Cline?"

"Yeah."

"*Ew*. Did you tell your brother?"

"Of course, but he wouldn't listen to me." I squinted my eyes. "Maybe we could break up the wedding. Don't they have one of those 'if anyone has objections' parts?"

She laughed. "I would never leave the island alive."

I laughed with her. "Me neither."

We continued discussing how we could sabotage the wedding, the trip to the island, and her mother's and my father's plans. We reminisced about elementary and middle school, people we knew, and funny things that happened. As the sun was coming up, we fell asleep.

I woke up to the sounds of her roommates in the kitchen and checked my phone. It was mid-morning. Elle was still snuggled in my arms, but her head was lying back enough that I leaned down and touched my lips to hers. She moaned and opened her eyes slightly. When she figured out what was happening, she placed her lips back on mine, and my morning wood wanted to jump through my pants and into her pussy immediately.

I leaned her back and kissed her deeply. She threaded her hands through my hair, and I involuntarily pushed my hard dick into her thigh. Fucking her mouth with my tongue, I remembered her taste from years ago. So sweet. I kissed down her neck and sucked hard when I got to the juncture of her neck and chest. She whimpered and threw her leg over mine, lining up my dick with her pussy.

Rolling on top of her, I pressed into her harsher but backed up. I leaned on my arms, checking her jade eyes for any resistance. She lifted her hips and rutted against me as I did her, then wrapped herself tightly around me like a monkey.

"I have to taste you." She nodded, and I slid down her body, tugging her shorts down as I went. She lifted her hips for me so I could rip them off while she threw off her top along with them.

I was staring at the most beautiful body I'd ever seen. Curves, lean lines, beautifully smooth skin... I wanted to tongue every inch of it. I wanted to come on all of it, claim it. I didn't want anyone to see this prize except for me.

She shifted in the bed and held her arms over her breasts as I gawked at her body. Remembering what I had slid down to do, I continued on my journey and opened her thighs. The scent of Elle made me grind my cock into the mattress to relieve some of the pressure. I imagined pounding into her.

As I slid my tongue up her slit for the taste, I

moaned deeply, which caused her to lift her hips, so she was closer to my mouth. I French kissed her clit, licking it and sucking, then held my tongue firm as I flicked with more pressure once I found my rhythm.

Occasionally dipping down into her hole with my tongue, she was writhing and panting, keening with pleasure. This was the best flavor I'd ever had in my mouth. Elle flavor. I loved eating pussy, but her pussy was like some delicacy. Crème brulee a la Elle. Lifting to my knees, I pulled down my pants enough to release my throbbing cock and masturbate.

As I began to fuck her hole with my stiff tongue, she rode my nose with her hips, gripping my head with her thighs. I switched and put my fingers inside her and began to pump her full while flitting my tongue back on her clit. "Ride my face," I commanded.

"That's it, please, please." She started to beg me.

"Mmm, you want to come?" I asked.

"Yes, please, please."

I moaned deeply into her clit, and her pussy clenched my fingers, throbbing erratically as she came on my hand and face. I sat up, stroking my cock violently over her body.

"Come on me, Levi. Come on my tits."

Oh, fuck. I licked a strip between her large breasts, and she shivered. I suckled one of her large pink nipples in my mouth, then the other, before squatting over her and pushing her cleavage around my dick so

I could fuck her huge tits. Each time I pushed up towards her beautiful face, she would bend down so her lips would suckle the head of my cock inside her mouth, or she would stick her tongue out to lick the tip.

"Dollface, I'm gonna come all over you."

"Do it. Fuck my tits, and come on me, Levi."

I pumped roughly and then exploded, cum shooting everywhere: her tits, her face, her tongue, her hair... I claimed as much skin as I could. She tried to gather as much as possible in her mouth. I let my head hang back. I hadn't nutted that hard in forever.

"Sorry I made a mess, but I had to paint you," I said to her, out of breath. "You look so beautiful covered in my cum."

She was licking up some from her face and laughing. "You're a dirty boy." She got up as I collapsed on the bed. "Don't go anywhere. I'm going to shower, but I'll be quick."

I wasn't going anywhere. I had no blood left in my brain to be able to leave. As I gathered my breath while lying on the bed, Elle's laptop lit up on her bedside table with a chat pop-up box. The only reason I looked was the picture of a naked chick in the website's header. Had Elle been watching porn before I got here last night?

Crawling closer to the screen, I saw it was a sugar baby website for rich guys. She'd been chatting with someone named DaddyJ007. I should have looked away... Yeah, screw that; I couldn't. I read their last chat exchange. Wow, who knew Elle could get that fucking dirty?

Why was Elle Townsend pretending to be a sugar baby for money? Didn't her dad have all the money? Was she threatened to get disowned every day like me? Who was this guy she was talking to? I scrolled through her chats. It was only him; there was no one else.

I was raging with jealousy. Fuck this guy. I could be her daddy. I wanted to be. I heard the water turn off in the shower and scrolled back on the website to leave the chat as it had been.

five

ELLE

While in the shower, I worried I let us go too far. I wasn't supposed to have an orgasm with a man unless I was going to marry him or something. At least had a commitment from him.

I was already planning to check Levi's social media accounts. It had been years since I did. He had never had a girl on his feed other than girls trying to photobomb his pictures, pretending they were with him. What if he had a secret girlfriend? Did he want children?

I put on a robe and went back into the bedroom. He was still there, lying on my bed, looking so fucking good. His penis was the best one I'd ever seen. I wanted it inside me, but that would have been way too far.

"Hey," I said.

He jumped and twisted around to see me as if I'd caught him looking through my panty drawer. "Oh! Hey."

"What's wrong?"

"Nothing," he said. He sat up and put on his socks and shoes. He came over to me and kissed my cheek. "Hey, my father is blowing up my phone. I'm pretty sure I'm disowned now. So, I have to head out. I'll text you."

"Oh, okay." Were we dating now? Was he my boyfriend? Was he going to come back later today and have sex with me? When he said he'd text, did he mean like today? I tried to play it cool. "I'll see ya."

He smiled sadly at me, then left.

The cold feeling of loneliness settled inside me again as he walked out of the apartment. This was why I had been avoiding orgasms with men for the last year or so. I hated this emptiness. Why did it have to be Levi? Why couldn't it have been with someone I didn't have a crush on? Someone with a smaller penis?

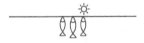

It had been two weeks since Levi and I had been together. Whitney's dreaded wedding weekend had arrived. My Louis Vuitton bags were packed, and a car would pick me up for the airport shortly. An oversized cardigan covered my white cropped T-shirt and baggy linen pants. Hair in a messy bun, I covered my head with my large headphones to drown out my real-world sorrows.

Levi hadn't texted like he said he would. Boys never did. I even made sure I unblocked his number about ten times. For the past two weeks, I stalked him on his social media, on Xavier's, on TRZ's feed, and on anyone's account he had ever tagged. I saw a lot of women with him in pictures at parties, but no one repeatedly. Maybe he liked to sex and split, like after Trent's party. Maybe I had been used. That thought made me cry a few times over the past week.

Everyone, even my friends, thought I was a player. They never knew how intense I got after a hookup. I told myself I was so affected this time because it had been so long since I'd been with anyone in person. The truth? It was because it was with Levi.

Solace was found in John, who was none the wiser regarding the Levi or Carter situation. I kept quiet about those events; he wouldn't have approved. John was quick to make me feel good about myself, complimenting my body and asking about my hopes and dreams. I learned he enjoyed reading old war history books and exercised daily in his home gym. Once, a woman's voice interrupted us when he talked, but he said it was his housekeeper.

John allowed me to use two fingers now when we made "daddy-daughter love" together on camera. He'd roleplay and say we couldn't be together in person because it was so wrong. The camera only showed his dick while masturbating; I never saw any more of him other than the office chair he sat in.

It was just as well. I'd probably get as obsessed with him as I was with Levi. I almost stopped checking Levi's accounts for a whole day when I had to leave for the trip. Perhaps Levi would irritate me so much that I wouldn't even care to check his socials when I got home. Maybe John and I would run away together.

Despite my headphones and audiobook, these things kept mulling through my brain while I sipped a cocktail in first class. Shirking the family's private jet, I planned a solo commercial flight to have peace before the chaos began. Unfortunately, the trip wasn't long enough.

A chauffeur from the airport dropped me off at the breathtaking resort. The weather was a bit overcast, but still beautiful. After checking in, a bellhop led me to my room. Mine was a walk-out on a corner with two patios that led to a long paddling pool that snaked around the first floor of rooms. A luxurious king bed filled the main room.

On a small table near a palm leaf embroidered loveseat sat a binder labeled "Whitney & Adam's Wedding Weekend." According to the itinerary, the festivities wouldn't start until a welcome cocktail hour that evening. The wedding ceremony was located on the beach the following day. However, the bride and groom-to-be would share a private romantic dinner alone. Just like Whitney to force everyone to come and then ditch. At least I wouldn't have to spend more time with her.

I changed into a strappy neon green bikini and tied a short black sarong around my waist. The bellhop had pointed out a few areas I wanted to explore, including the beach and the main pool. Slipping into a pair of black flip-flops, I headed out.

As I shut the door, the person in the room next to mine was also leaving his room. Of course, it would be Levi. He smiled brightly as he saw me.

"Hey, neighbor," he said excitedly. "You just get here?" His body was already tanned, skin the kind that picks up Vitamin D by being near a window. He wore those tiny navy blue swim trunks that showcased his muscular legs. At least he wore a Northview University T-shirt, so I didn't have to drool over his abs.

"Yeah."

"Me, too. You going to the pool? I was heading there myself."

"Um, yeah." *Great.* If he took his shirt off, I didn't know if I would be able to stop myself from being on him. Why was he being so friendly after ghosting me?

We wandered to the pool and chatted about our flights and treks from the airport. He reminded me of our weekend plans for sabotage, and I laughed. I wished he didn't, but Levi always put me in a good mood.

As we rounded a corner, my older sister, Elizabeth, and my aunt, Whitney's mother, ran toward us in a panic.

"It's off. It's off. Turn around and pack up," Elizabeth demanded.

"What happened?" I asked.

My aunt was crying and ran down the hall with a dismissive wave of her hand at me. Elizabeth stopped to talk with us—well, she mainly ignored Levi. She spoke as if she was trying to contain herself from sharing juicy gossip, but I knew she thrived on it.

"*Adam*," she looked to Levi as she said this, "called off the wedding. We don't understand why, but Whitney is devastated. We're all flying back with her on the jet. Mom's trying to calm her and Aunt Kim. Emilia's arranging our flights."

"But I just got here."

"Well, Whitney needs your support. Quit being so selfish. For once." She hurried off.

I looked at Levi. He was reading his phone, then held it to his head. "Yeah?" He paused. "I heard... Well, honestly, I'm proud of you. Nah, I'm staying. Get my money's worth... Do you need me? Okay, then. Take care, bro. See ya."

Levi ended his call. "Guess my brother finally wised up. You aren't staying?"

There was no way I wanted to go on a plane with

my mother, my sisters, my aunt, and my cousin. I could not think of a more miserable trip. If I stayed, I would never hear the end of it once I got home, but that was two days away. Spending a weekend with Levi? That sounded like it could be insanely fun. "No, I'm staying."

He relaxed and smiled. He grabbed my hand and tugged, saying, "Good. Let's get drunk."

Relaxing in the pool with our fourth round of fruity drinks, Levi and I were in fits of laughter, making it hard to breathe. My oldest sister, Emilia, approached us, her blond hair frizzed from the humidity. "We have been looking everywhere for you. What are you doing?! We're leaving in like an hour. Whitney is destroyed by what Adam did." She glared at Levi, who started cackling and back floated away.

"I'm not going. I'm staying here."

"No, you're not. Get out of the pool, Elle. Quit being so egocentric."

My dad strolled up to us on the side of the pool. "Hey, you guys look like you're having fun."

Levi yelled (slurred), "Willll! Hey, Mr. Townsend!"

I giggled and snorted. "Hi, Dad."

"Dad, she's drunk and not getting out of the pool." Emilia threw her hands on her hips.

"You're staying then, Elle?" My dad would save me, I hoped. If my mom wasn't around, he could get by with it. If Veronica walked up to us now, my life would be over.

"Yeah, I'm staying. Levi is here with me."

Dad smiled. "Oh, good. You take care of my little girl, Levi Joseph. You two stick together. Don't talk to strangers. No taking candy from anyone."

"You got it, Mr. Townsend. I'll take *gooood* care of her." Oh, geez. The way he said it made it sound so dirty, and it didn't go unnoticed by Emilia as she tsked at him. My father huffed a little laugh.

My dad squatted down to the pool to kiss me on the cheek. Then he pulled Emilia away by the shoulders while she said, "You let her get by with everything. That's why she's the way she is." I turned and rolled my eyes at Levi, who swam back up to me and put his arms around my waist.

He leaned in to kiss my neck, and I pulled back. "What are you doing?"

"Taking care of you; I told your dad I would. You looked like you needed to be kissed." I splashed him. He splashed me. "Do you not?"

"I just... what's going on with us?" Before I could completely regret asking, Levi's brother approached us poolside.

"Hey, man." Levi looked from me to Adam.

"Hey."

The pause between them was so great that I swam away to give them privacy. The mixologist at the pool bar had our next round waiting for me. While watching Levi and Adam, I sipped my fruity drink on the stool in the water.

Adam appeared sad, naturally. Levi seemed relaxed, occasionally floating on his back while they talked. Some of Adam's friends ran up, put their arms around his shoulders, and dragged him away. Adam head-nodded goodbye to Levi.

Maybe it would be a mistake to stay. If Levi was expecting us to have sex and be casual about it, I couldn't do it. I'd have to tell him. I think he would respect my boundaries. We could be friends. We could make this a friend's trip.

He swam up to take the seat next to mine. "This seat taken?" He grabbed his drink and sipped on it while smiling at me with his eyes.

"Is Adam okay?"

"Yeah, he will be. His buds are taking him to another resort nearby. He didn't want to stay at this one. Understandable. My father's pissed off and has left the island already to talk with our lawyers. He's never mad at Adam, so this is a new experience for me."

"I know the feeling."

Levi turned to me as if I had discovered the cure for a rare disease. "Yeah... Yeah, you do." His gaze was so intense that I sipped my drink to see if he'd look away, but he was lost in thought.

To shake off his gaze, I said, "Um, it's almost dinner time. Any idea which restaurant you want to go to?"

That broke his stare for a moment. "Huh? Oh,

dinner. Yeah. I am starving."

The bartender overheard and interrupted, "Mr. and Mrs. Joseph? You have your scheduled candle-light dinner on the beach this evening."

Levi grabbed my hand on the bar while I said, "Who? We what?"

At the same time, Levi said, "Oh, that's right. What time is that again?"

"I believe at seven, sir."

Levi leaned over to kiss my cheek. "Yep. Okay, Whitney... we will meet back up at seven for dinner. Want to head back to the rooms to get ready?"

As we headed back, I looked at Levi for an explanation. "They think we're Adam and Whitney. The whole thing's already paid for. We can really live it up on this trip, dollface. Honeymoon suite tomorrow. *Ooh!* What if we get a wedding cake?" Levi looked like that kid sharing his Kit Kats with me again.

"Should we do that?"

"Why not? Your cheating whore of a cousin's father already paid. Someone may as well get to enjoy it."

"You're right, *Adam!*" It sounded like a good time. No classes, booze all day... One bedroom tomorrow, though. Maybe there would be a living room sofa. Could friends sleep in the same bed? Could I sleep in the same bed as Levi and not have my pussy acciden-tally caress his huge dick?

"And we can check out as *us*, save ourselves some money," Levi continued.

"My dad paid for my trip," I said, and a shadow came over his face.

"Yeah, I'm sure he did." He turned to go to his room. "Come knock on my door when you're ready."

I dressed in a floral maxi dress and strappy sandals. After scrunching my hair into beach waves and applying minimal makeup, I knocked on Levi's door. He opened it and grabbed my hand, but held me at arm's length. He shook his head and said, "You're so beautiful, the most stunning woman alive, hotness." He looked sexy in his linen white shirt untucked over khaki pants. "Come on. I'm sober now. Need another Tutti Fruity or whatever those things were called."

As we walked toward the main hotel, away from our rooms, a concierge asked Levi if he was "Mr. Joseph." He led us to the beach, and I gasped as we approached a circle of palm trees hung with glowing lanterns and swags of exotic flowers. There was a white-clothed table set for two. Rose petals surrounded the table area, along with lit candle globes. The setting sun created a romantic backdrop, and the sound of the waves immediately put my nerves at ease.

Still clutching my hand, Levi led us to the table and pulled out my chair for me. We were served drinks and an appetizer while we gossiped about the day's excitement.

With two drinks in and the sound of the ocean, I felt confident enough to say what I needed to. "Levi, I'm sorry but I can't do casual sex. If, if that's what you wanted this weekend. With me. I mean, I don't think I can." I kept talking because he was staring at me without blinking.

"Oh." He furrowed his brow and looked at the table. "Huh."

"Is that what you wanted? I'm sorry."

"No. Not at all. I thought maybe that's what *you* wanted." Levi took a bite of his food.

"What? No, no, I can't do casual. I'm not good at it."

"Oh. Huh. Have you ever dated anyone before?"

I sighed and dropped my fork on my plate. "Look, I know the rumors about me. I get it. You thought I'd be an easy lay this weekend, a fun hookup. Sorry to disappoint—"

"Whoa! No, I don't give a shit about all that. I haven't dated anyone myself, is all I'm saying."

"Oh... Yeah?" I ate a bite, and he wasn't talking. I didn't understand what was expected of me. "So, friends then?"

Levi spat out his food. "Friends? With you? Uh, no." Now I was the one confused. He paused for a long time, sipping his drink and contemplating before he continued. "Want to try?"

"Try what?"

"Try *dating* or whatever. I mean, we are getting married tomorrow." He grinned. "We're on this romantic dinner. This could be our first date."

"You want to date me?" No one had ever taken me on a date before. Tears sprinkled my eyes, but I didn't want to scare him off, so I squelched them.

"I'm the one who told you I've had a crush on you since first grade. Yes, Elle, I want to date you. Would you be my girlfriend?"

"I've had a crush on you, too." His jaw dropped, so I quickly said, "Yes, I will be your girlfriend."

"Awesome, so sex after this?"

"Why after?" I teased.

Levi shook his head. "You're so fucking sexy... get over here."

Elle stood up from the table while I grabbed her waist with one arm and held the back of her head with my other, threading my fingers through her long, blond locks. Her light eyes danced in the candlelight before I devoured her pert mouth.

I needed her. I'd been avoiding this, but I couldn't any longer. My father wanted me to date? To settle down? There was only one woman in my mind to fulfill that role, and she was melting in my arms right now with the scent of vanilla and orchids blowing around us. I tried to savor the memory to write it in a poem later.

Grabbing her underneath her round bottom, I lifted her into my arms. Her legs wrapped around me, her long dress catching on my knees. I sat her on the edge of our little table, pushed the skirt up, and slid my hands up her inner thighs, feeling the wetness on her tiny thong.

"I don't have a condom here," I panted in her mouth, closing my eyes.

"I-I'm clean. Red Night test... I haven't been with anyone in, like, over a year." When I opened my eyes, our foreheads pressed together, I backed up, and she narrowed her eyes and pursed her lips.

Huh. Elle Townsend hasn't been with anyone in over a year? Maybe it was all just rumors. My vision flashed to her tight hole stretched to its maximum around my thick cock. "I've never done this without one. I haven't been with anyone in a while. Not since I got tested a couple of weeks ago."

"You're my boyfriend." Her face filled with lust. "Please, Levi. Please fuck me bare."

I groaned. I shoved her panties to the side and unzipped my pants, taking out my hard cock. Lining up, I slid the end through her wetness repeatedly. She leaned back on the table and moaned. Here it was. I was about to get everything I had wanted since I was a kid. Teasing her tiny entrance with the tip of my cock, I dipped in and out, in and out. I wanted her to understand the girth she was dealing with. She was tight as fuck.

"Please, Levi..."

Thrusting in some inches at a time, I eventually filled her and held myself there before I came too soon. Her hot, wet tunnel fisted my dick so snugly that I never wanted to leave. It's where I belonged, and the look of ecstasy on her face as she yelled when I entered made me think she felt the same way.

Each warm fold within her felt as though it was welcoming me home. It soothed some deep pain within me in a way I couldn't understand. Every secret hope I had for finding someone who's soul mirrored my own was hidden in Elle's body and I had just unlocked her. Her wetness was a salve to the burns of isolation, of not feeling wanted or good enough.

All this time I had waited for her. And now I knew the agony of not being with her had been worth it just to find this moment of paradise.

She leaned back until she was lying on the table. I held her long legs together up in the air and stood straight to fuck her. Punching my hips repeatedly, her hands gripped my thighs whenever I was close enough for her to reach, like she couldn't stop touching me. I understood her craving. Needing in deeper, I spread her thighs and scooted her forward on the table, her ass hanging off. I was losing grip with my feet in the sand, so I needed to hold her closer. From this angle, I was all in. The feeling of my cock being so close to her womb with no barrier made my balls tingle with the anticipation of release. I didn't give a fuck if I got her pregnant. In fact, I welcomed it. Take that, Warren.

"Hotness, I'm gonna come. I'm gonna come inside you." I panted out to her. "Come with me. Can you?"

"Yes, yes, daddy." She inhaled quickly as she said it and checked my reaction with half-lidded eyes.

I was sure she was saying this half out of habit. I'd read her chats with that creepy old dude. I wondered how long she had been with him or if she had feelings for him... That made me start ramming into her harder.

"Yes, I am your daddy now. No other daddies for you, okay?" I took one of my hands and spanked her ass cheek hanging off the table.

She arched into me and leaned up on her elbows.

"You hear me, dollface? You're my little girl, and I'm your only daddy." I spanked her hard. The rage of jealousy was making me want to hurt her with my dick, so she never forgot the feeling of me inside her.

"Yes, daddy."

"Fuck!" That name was doing something to me. "Come with me." She sat up to put her arms around my neck while I pushed in fully and came. Her pussy was clenching down on my cock as she went with me, milking me. I'd never felt the sensation of spurting ropes of my hot cum inside a pussy raw. I wanted to do it again as soon as I could.

As I held her there, I leaned forward to kiss her and drained my cock inside of her as much as I could. "I gotta do that again."

She laughed against my lips and said, "Me, too."

"I also don't want to get kicked out of the resort." I stood her up, let her dress fall, and then fixed my pants. Grabbing her hand, I led her back to our rooms, abandoning our dinner.

When we arrived at our hall, I pointed to our doors. "Which one?"

"Mine?"

We ended up fucking all night in her room. I took a break to get room service at one point. My appetite was ravenous after all our bodily workouts. Fortunately, the room had one of those boxes where the concierge could deliver the food without us opening the door.

By morning, my cock was spent; I had no cum left to inject inside her. We slept until late morning, tangled together in the sheets. The open doors to her patios kept us cool in the beach breeze.

She rolled over and looked at me with her morning sex hair. "What's on the agenda?"

"Pina Coladas on the beach until we can't see straight. In one of those beach beds, so I can fuck you again when no one's looking. Also, I think we can finagle the wedding reception food tonight if we play our cards right."

She kissed my neck, and I hugged her to me. "That sounds like an amazing plan."

After showering together (and fucking again—my cock recharged with cum), changing, and strolling to the beach, we found a nice cabana to chill on. We spent the day laughing about everything. I loved hanging out with her, even when my dick wasn't inside her, though I did love that, too. It was the best vacation of my life. I never wanted it to end. Waiter after waiter brought us drinks, so we always had two in hand.

"No way!" Elle flipped to her stomach so she could look at me better.

"Yep. You wanna see it?"

"Yes! Of course!"

I pulled my phone out and opened the videos. I showed her ours from eighth grade in Trent's bedroom.

"I cannot *believe* you still have this." She was focused on the video. "Wow, we looked hot together. Do you still watch this?"

"Hotness, I would be embarrassed to say how many times I've watched that video through the years."

She leaned over and kissed me. "We should update it."

"Huh?" I was plastered. It was hard to concentrate when she looked like that in a bikini, her nipples peeking over the tops of the triangles covering them.

"We should make more videos together." Her green eyes twinkled, and her hair whipped over her face in the slight ocean breeze. I turned on my side to shield her.

There was only one correct reply here. "Absolutely."

As she was leaning in to kiss me again, a staff member approached. "Mr. Joseph? It is almost time for the ceremony. Are you okay to proceed?"

We stopped kissing and gazed at each other.

"Yeah, we'll be there. Where is it again?" I asked in a daze.

"Just down the beach, sir. If you walk that way," he said while pointing, "you'll see the canopy all set up for you. When you're ready, the coordinator is at the end of the aisle." He walked off.

"What are you doing?!" Elle looked amusingly shocked.

"Let's do it. Let's do the ceremony. We'll get good food and good music. They're moving us to the honeymoon suite tonight. May as well go for it." Why not? Elle was awesome. My father wanted me to settle down, get married. I could show up Adam for once.

"You're crazy!"

"Yeah, crazy fun. Come on!" I sat up, grabbed her hand, and led us toward the wedding ceremony. "Oh, wait! I have rings! We have to go to the room to get them."

"Levi, you're insane." She was still holding my hand and smiling.

We went hand-in-hand to my room; I had to help her avoid stumbling while she walked. "Look, fuck Veronica Townsend. She'll be so mad she missed controlling your wedding. Will loves me, which will irk her even more, but she won't be able to stop bragging about you landing a Joseph, Warren Joseph of Cardell Enterprises' son." Damn, I made so much sense for a drunk person. I even sounded sober.

She seemed to consider. "Those do sound like good reasons... What's in it for you?"

"Fuck Warren Joseph. Plus, I think Will would give his son-in-law a job once I get disowned."

She laughed. "Okay. Get the rings. I'm in."

I grabbed the ring box Adam had left for me, his best man, and made sure the diamond band for Elle and the silver band for me were inside. "Let's go get married!"

The ceremony took place on the beach, facing the water. The sun was bright, creating sparkles on the waves. I was in my swim shorts with a lei of flowers around my neck, no shirt, and Elle had on a white bikini with flip-flops. I pulled a flower from my lei and put it in her hair.

There was a photographer taking pictures of us as we exchanged our vows. I stopped the officiant, knowing I was slurring my words, but didn't care. "I have something to say first. Hang on."

Clearing my throat, I quoted E.E. Cummings to her before I took my vows. "Elle Townsend. You are somewhere I have never traveled, gladly beyond any experience. Your eyes have their silence. In your most frail gesture are things which enclose me or which I cannot touch because they are too near. I do take you to be my wife. To have and to hold. From this day forth..." I finished my vows, and my cheesy lines must have worked because she teared up. Or maybe she was just wasted.

Elle tasted like Pina Coladas when we kissed, our first as husband and wife. I picked her up and was going to carry her off to her room, but the concierge stopped us, saying he needed our signatures for the license, then took us to the reception hall. He slipped me the key to the honeymoon suite and told me they had moved the items from our rooms to the suite.

"I want cake first, how 'bout you?" I asked as soon as we entered the large open-air hut filled with tables decorated with flowers. Hmm, at least Whitney had good taste. I spotted a two-tiered white iced dessert standing alone on a table near the buffet. There was a little wooden couple figurine on top.

Elle walked behind the cake. "Hell, yes. That looks amazing."

"Does it? You can have the first bite. Here." I took a handful, fed it to her open mouth, and then shoved the rest on her face. She gathered a handful and threw it at me. Fine, if that was how she wanted to play...

We destroyed one layer of the cake in our fight but ate the rest. I was stuffed, but the buffet looked good, so I kept eating. The waiter made sure our drinks were always full. Elle laughed so hard at one of my jokes that she fell out of her chair onto the floor, and I snapped a picture before I helped her into my lap.

I took our first picture together as she sat on me and posted it to my social media feed, pronouncing our marriage. "Here, since you're having such a hard time eating, I'll feed you." I put some chicken on my fork and fed it to her, her lips wrapping around the tines. I imagined her mouth around me instead of the utensil. She must have as well, as she writhed her hips into my hardening dick.

"That's it. Honeymoon time."

We practically ran to the suite. I almost noticed how nice the room was, but I focused more on getting her out of that tiny bikini and onto my cock. I untied it and pushed her towards the king bed. As she stood next to it, I knelt and licked her cunt as she moaned and rode my face. *Fuck*, I loved to eat her pussy. Before too long, she cried out and clenched my tongue.

"On your knees. Suck." I stood, threw off my shorts, put my phone on the bedside table, and held my dick out for her. "Wait, let me record this." I set the phone up to record her blowing me while she smiled seductively.

She knelt and licked the tip, then plunged to take me entirely down her throat with a thick swallow. "Oh, fuck." Elle knew what she was doing. She suckled my balls, licked my taint, and even dipped her tongue to rim my asshole until I almost came on her face. "Stop, stop, stop. *Stop*." I was having difficulty standing, all the blood rushing into my cock. I crawled onto the bed, head on a stack of pillows.

"Come ride this dick. I'll get a good shot for us." I picked up my phone from the table and pointed it between my legs as she situated herself there, facing my feet. She turned slightly to smile into the camera and backed up on my cock. She slid down slowly, and we both groaned at the sensation. "Mmm, wife, show me how much you want your husband inside you."

And she did. She started bobbing on my cock with her pussy like no one had before. The video was hot. Best porn I'd ever seen. I got a front-row show of her round butt and tiny waist working me up and down. Holding the camera with one hand, I put my thumb against her asshole with the other. I'd had enough when she threw her hair back and came all over my dick while swiveling her hips.

"All right, let daddy take care of you." I set up the camera on the bed to fuck her from behind while her face was in the foreground. "Look at the camera while I pound you." I loved seeing Elle's beautiful sunlit face while I thrust into her fully. She gasped; her expression shocked at being spread so wide by my thick cock. Whenever she'd try to close her eyes, I'd spank her until she opened them. "No, look at yourself. Shit, dollface, you look like I've fucked you so hard you've been brainwashed."

She was moaning and bouncing back off my dick

so hard the slaps were probably audible down the hall. "So big... So big... Levi, you're so fucking big." She was panting out. I squeezed my hand underneath to rub her clit so she could come again. "Oh, daddy. Levi!"

"That's it, my little girl. Take daddy's cock and cream all over it again." After she did, I moved the phone to the dresser. I grabbed her around the waist and lifted her off the bed, wrapping one of her legs around me so I could pound into her while standing. She began to hump my dick and went crazy on it. "Fuck, you love taking this dick, don't you?"

Elle's face was filled with utter bliss. "Yes, yes, yes, I do." Wow, this girl loved to fuck. I was so glad I wifed her. It was my best decision ever.

I grabbed her other leg so she was wrapped around my waist. She flew off my cock with each bounce, then slammed back down onto it. It didn't take long before I would lose it, especially once she came down and started grinding herself on me. "Levi, give me your cum, please."

"You want me to come inside you?"

"Please. Please, Levi, come inside me."

I appeased her and erupted within her walls while she rubbed her clit on me. As I did, I felt her come again, and I fell with her onto the bed with utter exhaustion, elation, and intoxication.

S heer throbbing pain invaded my skull as the sunlight streamed through the open patio doors of our suite. Pulling a pillow over my head, I groaned in search of any relief. I wondered how far away a trash can or the toilet was so I could vomit. A stiff leg kicked my shin.

"Ouch!"

Levi's bedhead was incredible. His wavy locks were crazily spread over his head in all directions. His eyes were blackened with two nights of poor sleep and drunken depravity. "Fuck, sorry. Damn. What time is it?" Looking around, he said, "This doesn't look like your room."

"We're in the honeymoon suite, remember?" I hoped the front desk had some miracle hangover cure.

"Yeah..." He sat up to get his phone and poured a

glass of water from the side table. The sheet slipped down to reveal his tanned, toned chest and exposed the stubble of his pubic hair above his morning erection. After taking a sip and glancing at his phone, he handed me the glass. It was refreshing and appeased the squeeze behind my eyes.

"Oh, shit. We're married. We got married." His expression of fear made me feel the same, as if he was suddenly regretting all his decisions. "Huh. Never done that while drunk before." His body slid back down into the bed as he stared off.

"You've never been married before? Well, I do it every Tuesday." I handed him the glass back. Maybe he was regretting this.

Oh, Elle, what have you done to yourself now? So desperate to orgasm with a man and make him commit to you, and he instantly regrets it.

I was falling for Levi. I'd always had a crush on him, and if he said anything about remorse, I didn't think my heart could ever survive. I shouldn't fall in love with my husband.

As if sensing my internal struggle, Levi leaned over, held my head in both hands, and kissed me. "Sorry, morning breath. I'll be back." He jumped off the bed and ran to the bathroom naked, tight butt muscles twitching as he did. His breath was pretty tasty; it was all him, Levi-flavored amazingness.

I heard the shower in the bathroom and debated joining him there. This was awkward. I wasn't sure what I should do. Did he regret this? Was everything okay between us? Was he just wasted during the ceremony and didn't know what happened? Was he scared and trying not to hurt me? Should I go to him in the shower?

I turned over on my stomach again to put the pillow back over my head, but his phone buzzed on the bed next to me. As I glanced over, several text notifications popped up on the screen rapidly with things like:

> Father: If you're not here this afternoon...

> Father: The lawyers already scheduled it...

> Father: You're not leaving the premises...

> Father: Serious, Levi. It is over...

> Adam: Father is rampaging, Levi.

> Adam: The plane is there. Better go...

> Adam: He knows. I'm heading there...

> Adam: I think he has a priest...

Wow. And I thought my family was screwed up. I checked my phone, which had messages of expected disappointment from my mother and sisters. Most called me selfish, "can't believes", and "how dare yous." One from my father said to have a great time, enjoy my vacation, and call him if needed.

Levi shuffled out of the bathroom with a towel wrapped low around his hips, showcasing his Adonis belt. He was drying his waves with another towel. I wanted to hump him. His phone started ringing. Adam popped up on the caller ID before I handed the phone to him.

"Hey." I heard some panicked voices yelling in the background. "Shit. Okay. When?" Levi eyed me before sitting down on the bed, back to me. "Tomorrow, but I'll pack. Adam... actually, let me handle this one. No, seriously." Levi huffed a sigh. "I'll see you then." Levi didn't move for a bit.

"So, sounds like you need to go?"

He turned to look at me. "When are you leaving?"

"My flight was scheduled for this afternoon."

Levi nodded and took a big breath in. "Yeah, I need to head out here in like 15 minutes." His face softened. "Elle, I gotta handle some things with my father, but when I get back, I'll find you, okay?" He slid over the bed to me and sucked my lips with his, biting my lower lip until I whimpered. Levi rushed around the room, getting dressed while gathering his stuff and throwing things into his bags.

Heading to the bathroom, I turned on the shower, holding my hand under the stream until it warmed enough. I heard the door open, then shut. Running back to the bedroom, I found it empty. Levi had gone.

In the shower, I sat on the floor tiles and cried, letting the water wash away my tears.

Worse than not being wanted was being married to someone who didn't love me.

When I returned to the main room in my robe, I saw a small piece of paper lying on my phone. Levi had scrawled a note on it that read:

Eyes like jade flow through me
Molded by the force of truth
Wandering without even trying
Until I was freed by you

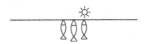

Veronica's Botox was wearing off. There was a furrow between her eyes and a crease on her forehead as she paced. Elizabeth stood to the side, facing the window. I swiveled on the kitchen bar stool, rocking myself. My sunglasses were still on.

"I guess I should have expected this. You've always been self-involved. But this was the worst day of Whitney's life. Your family needed you, and you abandoned us. Do you know how that looks to the Wades? To all the guests? We returned here and got off the family jet without you. There were local photographers, Eleanor! How do I explain to the readers of the

Northview News why our youngest daughter doesn't support her own family?"

I hated it when my mother used my full name. I was named after her mother, my grandmother, who (when she was alive) was twice as controlling as Veronica Townsend and always told me I was fat.

My mind raced with a million different ways I could answer her questions (Because you're a bitch. Because I don't support you. Because I've never felt a part of this family. Because I was getting railed by the best dick I've ever had.). I chose a reply that would allow me to continue living. "I'm sorry. I should have been there."

Elizabeth replied, "Yeah, well. It's too late for your apology. And we are not the ones you need to apologize to. Our cousin hasn't eaten, hasn't slept... Elle, consider how she feels for a moment. I couldn't imagine if Barry left me at the altar."

"He didn't leave her at the altar; he left her before the altar. Besides, she had been cheating on him, so he did the right thing."

The horror on their faces as they turned to look at me was amusement enough, but the outbursts of rage that followed made me bite my lip to keep from laughing.

"How dare you accuse her of doing something—" my mother was speaking.

Elizabeth was yelling at the same time. "You have no idea what you're talking about—"

Their voices blended into a cacophony of high-pitched squawks, one voice barreling into the other. My father was somewhere in the house. Maybe he would rescue me. No, he never came out of his room when things were hot, not with my mother like this. I was alone.

"—the entire Joseph family. Those men are play-boys without any sense of dignity." I paid more attention as I heard my mother mention my husband's family.

"Well, you heard about their mother," Elizabeth snorted. "Ran off with the pool boy or something. Apparently allowed him to impregnate her. Hasn't been seen since."

"I'm sure that's why their youngest has slept with the entire town. Probably solely responsible for that syphilis outbreak last year," my mother finished.

My cheeks flushed. "Levi is a good man. Leave him out of this."

Elizabeth sighed as my mother shook her head and said, "Oh, Eleanor. Your little crush doesn't change who he is—who his family is. The curtain has been pulled back, and we see the Josephs for who they truly are now. I thought Warren was doing a good job keeping his boys in line after their mother left, but I'm not sure how comfortable I feel attending the club with those three able to visit anytime they choose. I'll have to talk with Cecily Smith and Millie

Cardell." She went to get her phone, probably to start her next plan of sabotage.

"You need to apologize to Whitney. Stop with your rebellious nonsense," Elizabeth said.

"I will call her. See if she wants me to come over."

"Thank you." Elizabeth paused before she left the room. "Oh, Elle? Barry's sister's half-brother is single. He's 35 and campaigning for mayoral office next year. We think you two need to meet. Mother agreed it was a good arrangement. She mentioned perhaps next week sometime." The look on my face must have made her keep talking. "You need to make this up to her," she said sternly.

Emilia entered as Elizabeth spoke her final words. "You talking about Andrew? Well, if not him, Dr. Forsythe is ready to date again. He's a widower and has two little ones. He said he'd love to have more! He's only, like, 43, so he can still reproduce. Mom said it would be a smart match, Elle." She patted me on the back with some sort of affection. "Don't slouch. You'll get a hump."

"I'll go call Whitney." I slid off my stool and started towards the stairs.

"Tell us when you're available for Andrew—"

"—Or Dr. Forsythe!"

I went to my old room and sprawled on the bed. The overwhelming urge to text Levi came over me, but I resisted. He said he would contact me when he dealt with his family. Maybe he was getting the same treatment I was right now.

I tried to call Whitney, but I was sent straight to voicemail; I left a message apologizing for not returning with her and asking if she needed anything. I texted her, but there was no reply. At least I didn't have to talk with her.

My father always made me feel better, so I got up to look for him. I peeked around in his man cave, workshop, and garage. He was not home. William Townsend was a peacemaker. The poor man was riddled with four argumentative women in his household; serenity was a rarity he could only enjoy in nature.

Loneliness filled my heart; there was no one I could turn to. No one I could tell about my new marriage. Returning to my apartment provided some respite. I chatted with my roomies, pretending I'd had a great time on vacation, then headed into the protection of my bedroom.

It had been days since I messaged John. He knew about the destination wedding. When I pulled up the sugar baby website, I saw his green icon, indicating he was online.

L'Sucre22: Hey, daddy. Are you there?

DaddyJ007: Yes, I've been awaiting your return. You said you'd get back today.

Turning on my camera, I started a video chat with him. I didn't care that I was only wearing black leggings and a ribbed tank top from my long day of travel, hair tied up in a messy ponytail; I needed a friend.

"How was your wedding?" John turned on his voice chat.

"Oh, it didn't happen. The groom called it off dramatically when we arrived."

"But you stayed..."

"I already paid for the vacation, so I stayed to enjoy the beach."

"By yourself?" John asked.

"I hung out with a childhood friend, actually. It was nice to catch up," I said noncommittally; I felt the need to change the subject.

"Was this a male friend?"

Playing the character of a sexy, young kitten had been my role with John until this point. The tide shifted as I felt the urge to reach out for comfort. I glanced at my phone. Levi still hadn't contacted me. "Yes."

I heard John sigh. "You don't seem happy. Did you not keep yourself pure for me? Did you act like a whore?"

A gasp left my mouth, but I quickly controlled my face. "If you're asking if I had sex with him, then yes. I've known him for a while, and he was nice."

"But not nice enough to be with you now."

"No. I guess not."

"This is why, angel, I wanted you to remain pure for me. I can take care of your needs. Not only physically, but I will be what you need. You wasted your chastity on this boy... I'm disappointed."

I burst into tears. Everything was too much. "I'm sorry."

"Oh, precious. Shh, shh. I want to be there to hold you. He does not deserve you. Your daddy is right here. Talk with me. Tell me what you need." John's voice was so calm and kind.

I shook my head and tried to calm myself, but couldn't speak.

"Did—did something else happen while you were there?"

Sniffing, I replied, "Like what?"

"You're crying. Did you give your heart to him? To someone else?"

"I'm not sure." I paused. "John, I may have done something really stupid, and I feel like you're the only one I can tell this to. I have no one else. Me and this boy... we got married there. Like in a rush, drunk— and when I woke up, he left."

John was quiet for a very long time before he spoke. "I think we should meet. I can help you figure out how to handle this. Obviously, this was a mistake. There are ways you can make it like it never happened; no one ever needs to know."

I nodded but knew I didn't want things to be over with Levi but did he? Was he ghosting me or busy dealing with the aftermath like I was? I wished he would call or text. I couldn't be the one to contact him first.

John turned his camera on, moving it from his fully clothed crotch to his face. Clean-shaven with short graying brown hair, his brown eyes were filled with caring sympathy. He was a very handsome older man, perhaps in his 40s. Underneath his tight white dress shirt, you could see the outline of his hard work in the gym.

"If you feel comfortable, angel, we could meet. I can see how sad he's made you. Let me help."

I smiled at my camera but still had tears in my eyes. "Thank you, John, for being so helpful and kind. I need to do something first, but I'll let you know if we can meet."

Seeing his face, I felt like I may be getting into the same kind of trouble. Things felt real between us now, like I could feel something for him. And I felt like I was cheating on my husband. "I need to go. I'll sign back in soon." I quickly exited the program.

> Hey. Wondering if you're getting reamed like me.

The text went undelivered as if my number had been blocked. I needed to hear from my husband. In a panic, I tried to call Levi, but a message said the number I was trying to reach was no longer in service.

Kinsley came and knocked on my door. "Elle? There's a delivery for you." I sighed and relaxed thinking about receiving flowers or candy from Levi.

When I opened my door, my roommate handed me a large envelope. "Here, a courier brought these for you." The papers were sent from a lawyer's office.

I thanked Kinsley and closed my door. When I opened the envelope, I tried to comprehend what I was reading. Through hazy eyes, I read the title.

They were annulment papers sent from Levi Joseph.

The noose Warren bound around my neck was soothing to me. Like finding my way home, the reassurance of my prison was all I had ever known. It was comfortable; it was where I belonged. And he reminded me as soon as I landed on the private plane he had sent for me.

I was greeted by a new security guard who refused to give his name. My new friend took me to my father's house, never touching me but moving in such a way that I knew I didn't have a choice. Choice was an illusion.

Adam and my father sat in his office. As I approached, the large man shoved me into the club chair across from the desk. I guess touching *wasn't* off-limits. "Who's this?" I jabbed a thumb in the big guy's direction as he hovered over me.

"Your new babysitter," my father said sternly, standing behind his desk while staring at his computer tablet. "That will be all for now, Lawson. Please wait just outside the door."

"Babysitter?"

"Yes. You need one, apparently." He turned the tablet around to show off the picture posted on my social media account of Elle sitting in my lap at our wedding reception. We had shown off our, well, Adam and Whitney's wedding bands and were laughing. *Damn*, we looked good together. And also completely shit-faced.

Adam darted his eyes at me to see if I would feel the appropriate amount of shame looking at the photo.

"I thought congratulations would be in order. You told me to settle down, get married... like Adam." Adam's head dropped.

"I told you to date someone respectable, not to marry a *whore*." My father slammed the tablet on his desk.

"Why not? You did."

My father came around his desk in a flash. He grabbed me by the throat, and I held him by his collar. I was much stronger. Adam tried to step between us to break things up. "Hey, hey. Wait. Step back. Father, come on. Levi, let him go."

Lawson popped back in, but we broke apart from one another. My father returned to his seat behind the desk and motioned with his head for the guard to leave again. I stood in front of the chair, not about to sit again.

Adam tried to calm things down by speaking to me like a child. "Levi, getting married to Elle," he glanced at my father, "without a prenup, or without consulting us... was a bit rash. We're worried that—"

"—that girl has been with everyone, even her father's associates, Levi! Do you understand what you have done to our family name? What if she's already with child, Levi? She could try to take all of your inheritance. Everything I have worked for stolen because you couldn't keep it in your pants." My father swiveled to face the glass windows behind his desk.

"What Father's trying to say is we need to fix this. Now, I'm sure you had a great time with her, and you could date someone like Elle—"

"—Unacceptable," my father interrupted and swiveled back around in his chair quickly.

"Compromising, Father. You could date someone like Elle, but there are other women out there who are more appropriate. We will set you up if you're looking to settle down. I think it's a good thing he wants to, Father. He's showing he's ready." Adam looked at me like everything he said made perfect sense.

"I'm not taking dating advice from either of you. I'm not dating Elle." They both looked at me with hope. "I'm *married* to her. She is my wife."

"Yeah, well, not for long," my father mumbled.

"What is *that* supposed to mean?" My whole body tensed.

"It means I have had the lawyers working on this since last night. It will be annulled."

"No, no way. I'm not doing that."

"Levi!" Adam shouted at the same time my father yelled, "Yes, you will!"

I waited to see how they were going to control this situation.

My father was the first to break the heated silence. "Here's what will happen. Lawson will take you to your fraternity house to gather your things. You will move back here and *stay here* unless attending a class. I have had your phone disconnected from service. There are filters installed on the internet here. These social media accounts," he pointed to his tablet, "will be deleted. You will not see Elle Townsend again. We need to let this die down."

"Or what?" I already knew what was coming.

"Or you will be on your own."

I walked out of the room. Adam followed me to our old bedrooms. He stopped me with a hand on my shoulder. Lawson was at the end of the hall, watching us. "Levi, you've never had a job. Think. You've almost graduated and will be getting your MBA next year. It's time to grow up." I started to turn away and walk into my room when he stopped me again. "Just play along. Do what he says. You can be free after."

I twisted under his grasp and snapped, "Free after

when, Adam? When will I be free?" I went into my room and slammed the door, locking it.

I quickly pulled out my phone, but Father had already disconnected the service. My laptop at the manor... I could message her there. My mind raced with ways to try to contact Elle, my wife. I opened my door, and Lawson stood outside of it. "You ready?" He merely nodded.

The drive over was awkward. Me sitting in the back of my father's Mercedes as Lawson sat up front with the driver. I was plotting out any possible way I could contact my wife before my father destroyed us. I even considered jumping out of the car and running on foot. Lawson didn't look too fast, but I could be wrong.

When we walked into my room at the Theta manor, I ran over to my laptop and opened it. Lawson shook his head and manhandled it away from me. "Come on, fucker. That's mine." He held it tight to his chest.

I sprinted around him and down the hall looking for Xavier, but he was gone, probably with his girlfriend. I hadn't interacted much with him since Marissa came into his life. Back in my room, I threw things into bags and carried them back to my father's Mercedes, where the driver was waiting. Lawson lumbered behind me with my laptop still in his possession.

Before I got in the car, I spotted Big G walking

from the stable garage to the house. "G! Wait up!" The big man turned to me. "Hey! There have been some... complications. Tell Xavier I'm staying with my father for a while. I don't have a phone right now. I'll be back for the meeting this week, though." I eyed Lawson as I spoke the last part. Big G followed my eyes to the large security guard and nodded in understanding before entering the house.

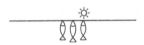

The week was torture. The only time I could leave my father's house was when I attended class with Lawson hovering behind me. He even stood outside the classroom doors. I saw Elle once and yelled to get her attention, but she kept walking, not seeing me. The Theta Rho Zeta meeting came and went, but I wasn't there. It was the first I had ever missed.

My father couldn't block my university email; I needed it for class. I sent Elle at least two dozen emails explaining what was happening, but never received a response. Worried she hadn't opened them, I typed messages in the subject lines.

Please hear me out. I need to see you.
I miss you. Please read me.
I'm trapped at my father's. Please send help.
I have no phone. Please respond.

I spent hours at night laying on my bed thinking about how perfect Elle was, remembering her hair, her eyes, her smile—trying to recall that sweet mango scent and how she looked when we exchanged vows. My journal was filled with little lines of poetry I saved for her if I ever saw her again.

Winter white sunshine flowing
Sparkling over me in waves
Orchid vanilla breezes blowing
In your arms, I've been saved

They were silly, not enough, but I worried I'd never get to share the words with her.

The longer time passed, the more I realized how much I truly wanted Elle. It wasn't just her body; she had such a kindness to her, a gentleness I craved. I remembered all the times we laughed together and hoped she thought of me somewhere, too.

As Halloween drew closer, I had given up on hearing from Elle. Maybe she had regretted what had happened. Perhaps she realized what a fuck up she had married and wanted it over. I pushed her from my thoughts because it was too painful to think of her. I was doing well going to class, keeping my head down, and my father satisfied.

Father was in his office the day before my next TRZ meeting. We had only spoken two days before when he gave me a phone saying, "this is for business and school only." The phone had a new number. None of my old contacts had been saved. He made sure all my social media accounts had been deleted and said he would check my call and text logs.

I needed him to grant me, his fully grown adult human son, permission to attend my fraternity meeting, maybe even possibly the Halloween party. "Father?" I asked as I knocked on his door.

"Enter."

I'd played this game for years. I had all the cheat codes and had beaten the levels several times. It was the final boss, who was a difficult beast. "Father, is it alright if I sit down?"

He nodded and pointed to the chair in front of him.

"Theta Rho Zeta is important for my future. I must show responsibility as an officer and attend the meetings. I wanted to ask you, sir, for permission to attend on Wednesday evening."

"You're right, Levi. You should attend. Lawson can wait outside in the car for you."

"Thank you, Father. These last two weeks have been a good lesson for me. I apologize for my behavior, my philandering, truly."

"Are you sincerely sorry, son?" Warren narrowed his eyes and furrowed his brow. He was suspicious, which he honestly should be.

"Yes. Being away from the booze and girls has helped me put things into perspective. I'm sober now and able to think straight. You and Adam were right. I should not have made such a rash decision to get married. It brings us all, our family name, down. I am sorry." Damn. My Oscar-worthy performance almost had *me* in tears.

"Well, if you are, you can start your apology tour by expressing your regrets for how you treated Samantha. I haven't had a chance to check in with my other dates, but I know Samantha was hurt by your behavior. She's having dinner here this evening." Ugh, that didn't sound good. I did walk out on her when she was crying.

He continued, "I thought it best for you to apologize before she starts throwing out accusations and wrecking your future. Make sure she buys your apology." He started to look away. *I'd make sure she felt my apology*. My father interrupted my thoughts. "Without your penis. She is not in the *respectable* club. Adam and I will find you a suitable woman soon."

"Yes, sir. I will be respectful." I paused. "Xavier and the guys want to play airsoft on Saturday... before the Halloween party. Is it too much to ask for me to attend? Could it be a test to ensure I have learned my lesson?"

My father took a deep breath and stopped. It took a long time for him to respond. "Levi, I know you like to say things you don't mean. It *is* beneficial for you to be around Xavier Cardell. Xavier's a good influence on you. And, of course, you'll be his right-hand man in the future. The game is fine. The party... We shall see about your party on Saturday afternoon. If you continue doing as well as you have been, then maybe."

"Thank you, sir." I turned to leave before he could change his mind. "Will I see you for dinner later, Father?"

"No, I'm dining out. Samantha will be arriving at six, and Lawson will be here to check there are no accusations thrown around and that you keep things... proper."

Samantha showed up for dinner wearing a designer gown with her hair done up. She looked good, but sad. I was wearing jeans and a TRZ T-shirt and dirty socks. I greeted her and brought her into the dining room. "Welcome. Please, have a seat." Lawson stood at the end of the room, a foreboding presence for an uncomfortable dinner.

"Thank you, Levi. Your father said you wanted to talk to me. After the way we left things, I didn't think you cared." I took my seat, and she moved her plate across the table to sit beside me. *Great.*

"It's all my fault. I apologize for getting involved and then leaving things as I did. You deserved better. I'm a stupid kid." I took a bite of my pasta. "Can we still be friends?" I didn't mean it. Samantha meant nothing to me other than a way to irritate my father.

Samantha placed her hand on my thigh and grasped it. "I was hoping this was a call for another reason." She raised her eyebrows and licked her lips. My mind flashed to the honeymoon sex I'd had with Elle, and I got sad again. Images I'd been trying to forget.

"I'm sorry. My father has forbidden me from doing anything with you. You know how he is. I believe he wants you all to himself." May as well fuck him over as much as possible.

Samantha sat up and said, "Yes, you said that last time. Right before we did it again—"

"—Yes, I said it the last time, but it is still true." Damn. I did say that before we fucked again. Had forgotten about that. Lawson cleared his throat.

"I thought you said that made you nut harder," she said quietly while glancing at Lawson. Well, it certainly used to. Things had changed. I only had one woman on my mind and knew nothing else would do it for me.

"Well, the truth is, I'm now with someone."

What I said was the wrong thing because her face crumbled and her shoulders sagged. Her eyes filled with tears. "You-you've never dated anyone before. What changed? Who is she?"

Looking at her made me wonder what I was ever doing with her. Or with anyone else, for that matter.

She wasn't Elle. No one was. "She's the love of my life. I'm sorry if that's harsh, but—"

"Was it that little girl you took that picture with? The one when you posted to your account? Does your father approve of her?" I thought she might cry.

This could have gone better. Who knew Samantha even followed my social media accounts? I didn't think she even cared. Clearly, I was wrong. "Um, yes. That was her. It was unexpected. I'm sorry, Samantha. I truly am." And now I was. I guess I had been callous.

She jumped up from her chair and bolted from the room. She left the door open as she fled. Lawson looked at me for a brief moment, then followed her.

Reeling from the exchange, I decided to do what I had planned for weeks. I was waiting for Lawson to get distracted. Quickly, I sneaked into my father's office and used the password I figured out by watching his fingers stroke on the keys sitting across from him, listening to his lectures on decorum.

I logged into his computer. I needed to message Elle on social media or somewhere, let her know I loved her and I was coming for her. Thought about trying to call her from the computer, but time was ticking.

My father's internet browser was already open. My whole body shuddered when I clicked on the program in the taskbar. Pasta rolled in my stomach, almost landing on the carpet in front of me, but I held it back.

The proof was now in front of my eyes. I had ignored it until this point. Like my father did with my mother. Like Adam did with Whitney. I should have accepted the cold, hard truth.

Elle Townsend was a whore.

nine

ELLE

"**P**lease, please, please, you have to go." Marissa was in that opiate-induced love phase of her new relationship with Xavier. It was annoying. The two were never apart. I didn't want to be around my friend and my childhood bully. Every time I was, I was reminded of Levi, and my heart broke a little more.

"Alright, I'll go. Not sure which costume to wear, though." Marissa had been begging me to attend the Theta Rho Zeta Halloween party. The only reason I planned to go was to give Levi his stupid annulment papers back. Signed. It would be the closure to a life-long mistake of a relationship. I hadn't wanted to annul our marriage, but obviously, he did.

It hurt more than I thought it was possible to feel hurt, knowing that my husband didn't love me, knowing he wanted out of our relationship without even giving it a try. It would have felt better if he were honest and *told* me he just wanted a good lay over his vacation weekend. But I couldn't think of it any longer because when I did, I'd start crying again.

None of my friends or family knew what I was going through. That was my fault; I didn't feel it was safe to tell anyone, especially if the marriage was being expunged. My mother would make me feel even more miserable than I already felt. I couldn't even get the words out to say it to myself, let alone my friends.

Instead, I kept up the façade of my party girl image. I went to all the parties and all the outings. I flirted with boys. I went to classes and did my homework. I went fishing with Dad. I was normal, according to everyone; I didn't let anyone see my pain because I didn't want to feel it. The only one who knew what was happening underneath was John.

Things were progressing in our relationship. We decided to meet in person at a restaurant (a very public one) in a nearby town. I didn't want him to know where I lived, so I gave him an estimate. He had not shared where he was from, either, but said he would fly into wherever I lived and choose a romantic spot for our first meeting.

I would have to get my costume together for the Theta party the following day. My first date with John was that evening. Maybe it was stupid not to tell my friends about it, but John was my secret, and I wanted to keep him that way.

Driving to the restaurant, I thought about my expectations for the date. Why had I agreed to meet him? Insightfully, I knew my despair over Levi had everything to do with it. John said he could help me strategize how to end the relationship with some good legal and emotional advice. I trusted that. He was wise and older; he understood this stuff. Plus, he always made me feel good about myself.

We had not masturbated on camera together since I returned from my trip. I thought we should either stop our online activities and end things or pursue a real-life relationship and get to know one another. The cam girl orgasms John had given me were too confusing. My brain wasn't sure how to feel about a man I hadn't met in person. So, I decided I wanted to give the real relationship option a try.

I worried that even being in a relationship wouldn't be safe. Levi and I were officially dating when he gave me the big orgasms, yet he broke my heart. Maybe the health teacher in high school was right: masturbation was the only safe sex. Except my purple dildo wasn't cutting it for me anymore. Whenever I used it, I'd think of my trysts with Levi and no one else.

The meeting location was a beautiful old white wooden farmhouse—a bed-and-breakfast. My heart thudded in my chest as I approached the outside. The place wasn't just a restaurant. That meant there were rooms for rent... like for sex. Was that why John had picked this place? Was I committing the same stupid mistake again?

For our date, I chose to wear a pale pink boatneck mini dress with ruffles at the bottom. Kitten heels decorated my feet and pearls adorned my ears. I wanted to look innocent, which I knew John liked, but also a little sexy. I left my hair down and fluffy.

As I stepped out of my car, I noticed him standing next to a black Mercedes. Wow, he was quite attractive, with taut arms and a sculpted jaw, more so in person than online. He smiled slightly as he saw me, brushed my hair off my shoulder, and cupped the back of my neck.

"Hello, angel." He leaned forward as if to kiss me, but hesitated to see if I wanted him to. I did not feel comfortable with that, so I pulled back, and he allowed me, sliding his hand from my neck down my arm and grasping my hand instead. It was very courteous.

"Now that we are together I'd like for us to hold hands, at least. You may greet me," he said demonstratively, not any different from the roleplay character he usually played. I didn't know what I was expecting, perhaps a less authoritarian person than the one he played online.

"Hello, John—"

"Ah, ah. You'll address me as your daddy. Unless there are others around."

"Oh. Hello, daddy." I smiled, and he bent down to put his cheek towards my lips. I kissed it.

"My little girl looks breathtaking. I love this dress on you, precious." He slid his other arm around my waist and led me to the front door of the restaurant portion of the house.

"I noticed this is a bed-and-breakfast... Was there something you were trying to tell me, Jo-daddy?"

John smiled down at me. "Yes, I do have a room here. But I chose this place because I heard it has good fried chicken. You will like it."

None of the patrons judged us as we were led to our private booth in the large dining room. I thought our age difference would make people stare, but they didn't. John did look young for his age, which I still didn't know. Was it rude to ask?

"John, I feel like I should get to know you better," I said after he placed our drink orders. John sat in the booth seat next to me, choosing not to take the one opposite.

"Sure, angel. What would you like to know?" He held one of my hands on the table and the other on my thigh, just underneath my ruffled dress hem.

"How old are you?"

John smiled. "I am in my early 50s. I hope that isn't a problem for you. My previous marriage ended a long while ago, and I would like to get re-married... and have children." He waited to see what I would say.

"I was worried you were married." I dodged the statement about children.

"There's been only one little girl occupying my mind for a long time now."

Our food was served, and John was right; the chicken was delicious. We enjoyed some small talk about the food, but John dominated the conversation as if he were lecturing me about everything he knew, which was a lot. He spoke about how to make perfect Southern fried chicken, about the history of the pre-Civil War era bed-and-breakfast we were in, about the way the cutlery on the tables was made... His knowledge was detailed and diverse.

John was fascinating to listen to, but it wasn't a conversation. I was his chosen audience, an object to be entertained. It became exhausting.

Toward the end of the meal, his expression turned serious. "We need to discuss the trouble you've gotten yourself into, but I think it needs to be a private conversation." He glanced around the dining room. "Let's head up to my room."

I slightly resisted as he took my hand to lead me from the booth. "John, I am not sure about that." I dropped my voice to a whisper. "I don't want to *have sex*. Not today."

John's face was caring as he said, "Oh, precious. We cannot make love today. You're involved in this... entanglement, so we'll need to ensure there are no other ties before we can engage in anything physically. It would not be prudent."

So the high moral act wasn't just a roleplay. At least I could use it to my advantage. "Okay."

After he checked in with the front desk, I allowed him to lead me to his reserved bedroom upstairs. It was a quaint room with a rounded bay window and a little bench underneath, making a quiet reading space. The king-sized bed filled the center of the room and was made with a patchwork quilt and too many pillows. Antique furniture dotted the rest of the room.

John sat us on the long cushioned bench at the end of the bed. Feeling more at ease that we were not on the bed itself, some of the tension began to leave my body. John turned more toward me and continued to hold my hand.

"I would happily have my lawyers review your case and give you some legal advice, but it is probably best to sign those annulment papers and get things done and over with. We can make it disappear as if it never happened."

He brushed the hair behind one ear. "Elle, angel, darling. Once you've been made pure again, I want to marry you and have children. I see now that waiting and attempting to court you has been an issue. You seem to have certain needs that you cannot control. I've tried to help you tame them, but evidently, you need your daddy to step in now."

I furrowed my brow. He wanted to marry me? And

have children? Purify me? "What—what does that mean?"

"It means I will make your decisions from now on. You don't need to worry about anything. Just let daddy take control." He stroked my hair. "You won't need to finish that useless degree. I'll need you to manage my household, and then we must get you pregnant as soon as possible after the wedding."

My hand resting in his was trapped. His body leaning into mine was a heavy weight. The door to my escape was so far away. "John—"

"—Ah, ah... daddy," John corrected.

"Daddy, I'm not sure getting married and having children is what I want right now. I mean, I'm technically still married."

"What you want no longer matters. As you've seen, your decision-making has led to poor consequences up until now. You know I will take excellent care of you. I plan to spoil you rotten, give you everything a woman could ever desire."

Fisting my hair into one of his hands and pulling on my hand that was gripped in his, he leaned me over his lap and held me tightly around the waist. "Now, we need to talk about your purification. I'm glad you wore this dress." He lifted the bottom of it. "And a pretty thong for me, it seems."

John spanked me harshly, and I lurched forward, yelping in shock. His arm was so tight around my waist that I couldn't squirm away. "We will commence with your first punishments for allowing your body to be used by other men." He whacked me again, and I tried to twist, but he was very strong. "Don't shirk from your punishment. These spankings will help purify you, but the surgery will be the final step before our wedding."

"S-surgery?" I squealed as he spanked me again.

"You will address me appropriately. Only speak if I ask you to do so." My ass was stinging when he smacked me again. "Angel, I have scheduled your hymen repair surgery so you can be pure for me again." *Spank!*

I was crying in fear. If I could get my feet to grip the floor, I could push against him enough to free my body. My little heel kept slipping on the rug. He held my arms behind my back, gaining a tighter grip.

"Yes, daddy. Spank me, punish me. Purify me. How many spanks do I deserve?" I sobbed. Trying a new tactic, I attempted to lower his guard and get him to think I was his, that he had me.

"How many does my angel think it will take until there are no other men she wants? Until she submits to daddy's will? Until you're sorry for being such a little slut?"

I wailed, "I only want you, daddy. It's always been you. I made a stupid little girl mistake marrying that man, allowing my body to be used. Please forgive me. I'll be pure for you."

It was working. With the hand spanking me, he

started groping my sore bottom. "Mmm, my little girl is so precious. Such a good girl for me. I want you to lie over the bed and pull down your panties. I brought a paddle in my luggage. I think ten swats will be enough for today. We can do more tomorrow. You need to understand that you deserve this."

My head nodded. He was going to let me up to go to the bed. As he released my arms and waist, I darted up and ran to the door, trying to unlock the doorknob quickly as he said, "Stop!" and marched toward me with purpose. His body loomed behind mine when I opened the door. I flew into the hallway, down the stairs, and out of the house.

"Stupid, stupid," I repeated to myself as I jumped in my car, locked the doors, and drove away from the restaurant. I even went a separate way and not in the direction of my town, just in case he saw where I was heading. Crying inhibited my ability to see straight, but I wasn't going to stop. Digging into my center console, I found some tissues and wiped my eyes while driving.

I was a very stupid girl. I should never have trusted some dirty old man on the internet... And why had I? My mother always made my decisions for me. She always told me what to wear, how to wear it, what to do with my body, whom to date... My sisters made excellent substitute teachers when my mother wasn't around.

Maybe I grew close with John because I thought

he would at least be better than Veronica Townsend at managing my life. Now, I was hurt and betrayed by a man I was so desperate to please. My chest ached at the thought of losing his guidance, his encouragement, at losing the man I thought he was. Tears fell off my cheeks and dripped onto my arms thinking of the loss of what could have been with John.

He was supposed to rescue me from my idiotic decision to marry Levi. Instead, he took our relationship and twisted it in a disgusting way. I was just a doll for him to play with and control.

John was paying for a fantasy, but I had been the one playing make believe.

All I wanted to do was call Levi, my husband, and have him hold me. Seek comfort within him. But he didn't want me. I had no one to turn to now. No one I could trust or rely on.

My friends would think I was insane for allowing myself to become a sugar baby. How could I explain it? My family was wealthy; I came from a good upbringing. Why would I entertain gross men for money?

Veronica would be appalled, and I would face constant criticism for years from my sisters. They would probably send me to an Abbey like in *The Sound of Music*. Shame and embarrassment flushed my cheeks at the thought of my father finding out what I had been doing. Dad was the closest person to me, and I couldn't tell him any of this. I would hate to disappoint him.

I thought Levi would be the one who wouldn't judge me, who would protect me. He hadn't even tried to call or text me. He had just sent the annulment papers straight from his lawyer's office. I had seen his first few emails but filtered the rest to my trash can so I wouldn't read them; I needed a Levi detox.

Now I was filled with sadness at the loss of him. The way he made me laugh, the way he made my body feel, the kindred way we felt about our families. I thought he understood my plight like no one else. I thought we were in this life together.

I guess I was wrong.

I t was Halloween, and I had not been "granted permission" to attend the party at TRZ. That was not enough to stop me, however. I finally dodged Lawson long enough to sneak out of my father's house and call a ride-share to pick me up outside our gated community.

I was done with Warren Joseph. His hypocrisy knew no bounds. If he caught me sneaking back in, so be it. My noose was ready to be loosened.

Dressed as a firefighter without a shirt, several ladies stared as I strutted to the kitchen to drink liquor with my boys. I caught a glimpse of Elle in the reception area dressed as a doll with a pink wig, large sunglasses, a leopard print miniskirt, and a tight T-shirt with "Barbie" written on it. She looked way too appetizing, but just glancing at her filled my body with so much rage that it felt like I'd just drank a cup of hot lava.

While taking shots, Mason asked Marissa if he could meet Elle. Growing up, he went to different schools than us, so he didn't know her. I turned him off quickly, saying she'd been around. I knew that would do the trick for him. Why I was trying to keep him off her when I should be over her was beyond me. She was just as disloyal as any woman.

I decided to return to my one-and-done ways. I just needed to find the right pussy to fuck. Hopefully, I would in front of Elle, so she had no doubt I was over her. Completely. No going back.

Unless she has a good explanation...

On my way to the dance floor to choose a fuck partner for the evening, Elle ran into me, her large breasts pushing into my chest. Why did she have to smell so good? I was about to yell at her to get out of my way when she shoved a folder of papers at me.

"Here's your paperwork, asshole."

"What paperwork?" I opened the folder, and a signed form titled "annulment" was inside. "Fuck. Is this what you want? You want a fucking annulment?!" I didn't think I could become more furious than I already was. Isn't this what I wanted?

"What *I* want? You couriered them to me the day after our wedding!"

"I did no such thing. Is this your and Warren's latest plan to fuck with me?" They were probably laughing together at my reaction when they came up with the plan—trying to plan other shit to mess with me behind my back, too.

"Who? What are you talking about?"

Several people tried to walk past us in the hall while we were yelling, hot in each other's faces. A few stopped for a moment to see what the argument was about or to make sure the girl was safe and I wasn't going to hit her or something.

Grabbing Elle's arm, I shoved her into the hallway bathroom. She acted innocent, like she didn't know what was happening. I knew. I had figured it all out. "You and my father. Scheming to fuck with me. How long have you been plotting this?"

"Plotting what, Levi?" Her brow furrowed, and she shook her head slightly.

"You're really going to act all innocent with me? You know, I didn't care who you slept with, Elle. I didn't care about rumors or even if you had, in fact, fucked the entire university. I just didn't expect you to fuck my father and try to, what, work with him to get my inheritance? Keep me in line? What was the goal there?"

"What in the *world* are you talking about, Levi?"

I huffed and turned around, but could still see her in the sink mirror. I set down the folder and ran a hand over my face, grabbing my chin as I turned to face her again. "I know about you and Warren Joseph, your little sugar daddy, sugar baby relationship. God, I can't even say it without wanting to fucking vomit." Elle paled to an even whiter shade. I gave her a moment to respond, but when she didn't, I continued. "So, what was the game you had? Figured you'd make me fall in love, then get me under his control? You need money?"

"You... how did you know about the sugar baby thing? I never said anything to anyone."

I shook my head. This is the question she chose to answer. "I saw your laptop that day in your room. Your daddy, ugh, *Warren*, messaged you. I wasn't spying. You know, I thought there was something wrong with you and me. I should have paid better attention. No woman can be loyal. You're all fucking cheating whores."

"Levi, I didn't cheat on you. The entire two days we were together, and I am not now. Why do you keep saying I'm involved with your father?"

"Because I know, Elle! I *know*! I saw his computer, saw his chats with you, fucking whore. Planning to meet him. The videos, the *pictures* of you on his computer. So many fucking videos and pictures. That *you sent him*!"

Elle started hyperventilating and sank to her knees in front of the toilet. "Oh, I think I'm going to be sick."

"Join the fucking club, sweetheart."

Elle burst into tears, sobbing. "I—I, please... Please, Levi. Show me a picture of your father."

What a strange request. She was on the floor crying, almost hacking up vomit, and wanted a picture of my father. "Don't you know what he looks like already?"

"*Please*, Levi. I never met him. You know that."

"I thought I did... I thought many things," I said sadly, quietly. She was hysterical, hiccoughing onto the floor.

"I didn't know."

"Didn't know what? That I'd find out about your little game?"

"Please, Levi. Do you have a picture?"

I decided to test her. If she was truly innocent and I showed her a picture of another man who was not my father, maybe she would feel relief, thinking it wasn't her daddy. I never posted pictures with my father; not even sure I had one. The country club's website had a photo of me and Adam with Steve Smith from a tournament the year before. I flashed the phone around and pushed it near her face.

"That's not him! That's not him! That's not John. It's not him. Levi, I have never met that man before."

I searched online for a picture from two Christmas' ago with Adam, my father, and me at the Cardell's party taken by the local newspaper. I showed her the picture and said, "This is Warren Joseph." Her face shattered into a million pieces, and she howled.

"No, no, no..." She hung her head. She was a broken doll.

I squatted down and put a hand on her back, gently rubbing. "You didn't know." She shook her head. I sat on the floor and pulled her into me. She sobbed, throwing her arms around me.

"Levi." She hiccoughed. "Levi, I never, ever slept with him. Never. I would *never* have been involved had I known, I swear to you." She sniffed. "He scared me."

I pulled her back to look at her. "What do you mean?"

"I started this stupid sugar baby thing months ago to avoid-avoid having casual hookups. I figured it would be safer. John, your father, bought out all the other daddies. When I told him about marrying you and getting the annulment papers, I was so upset... I never really revealed personal information until then."

"I didn't send them, Elle. I didn't want to. I couldn't contact you. He was controlling everything."

Elle shook her head. She told me about meeting him in person and why she did it. Then she told me what happened in the bedroom above the restaurant where they met. If I had any doubts about cutting myself off, that story solidified my decision.

Pulling off her sunglasses, I wiped the tears from her face. She looked embarrassed and put them back on. "My face is a mess."

I kissed her gently, briefly. "You're beautiful, doll-face." She leaned in and sucked my lips in with hers. I groaned. "Fuck, I missed you." I stood to get her up, but she stopped me and crawled to me on her knees. She lowered my zipper.

"I need you. Please, Levi." She looked at me so sweetly from what I could see behind her glasses. I held up my phone and started recording. I never wanted to forget any of these moments.

I wasn't returning to my father's house. If I did, I'd kill him. If he somehow trapped me, I wanted to have something of her. Something to replace the videos I may lose of us in Trent's bedroom, of our honeymoon.

"Hotness, I'm not letting you go." I pulled out my cock, but stopped her from latching onto it. "No more sugar baby. No daddies. No one else ever. It's only me, right?"

"Only you, Levi." She started sucking while I filmed, leaning against the sink. She would glance up at the camera, her perfect, plump pink lips suctioning down my shaft. She was an expert. My knees were getting weak; I wanted all of her.

"I don't want to come like this. Dollface, please. Let's go upstairs."

She got up, and we straightened each other up. I went to the door, which was partially open, and took her by the hand to show her to my room. As we stepped inside, we undressed each other. It wasn't hurried. I would take the time to enjoy her for as long as I wanted.

Tossing her wig aside, I put my face into her

golden locks and inhaled a nice, deep breath. Her scent flooded my memories, and I wanted to be back with her in our tropical honeymoon suite. We should have just stayed there forever, but here we were, finding solace in each other's bodies once again.

I snacked on her lips, then moved down her neck and chest to her nipples. Suckling one, I latched on as if getting my midnight feeding. Then I switched to the other while she arched her back and moaned into me. I laid her on the bed, continuing to nip, bite, and suck while flittering my tongue on her nipples. Grazing my fingers down her stomach, I slowly parted her pussy lips, finding her clit, gently rubbing it with two fingers. She whimpered and writhed.

Yep, I was taking my time. I slid down her body, parting her legs. She shuddered when I licked up and down her slit. I pried her thighs open when she pinched my head with her knees. She propped herself up on her elbows to gaze at me, and I met her expression of desire as I feasted on her juices.

My tongue could have tasted her twat all night, but my cock was getting eager and insistent, being so close to her scent and wetness. As much as I wanted to video this for myself for later, I also wanted to be present as much as possible. I decided to leave my phone where it was and be mindful.

Her legs parted for me when I knelt between them and scooted closer to join our bodies. I leaned forward to grasp her jaw so she would look at me. Slowly, I entered her a little at a time, pulling back slightly before tapping in repeatedly. Elle threw her head back into the pillow and squinted her eyes shut while gasping, forcing me to release her face. "I love this part," she whispered breathily.

"Me, too."

I began to pump her full with a steady rhythm. Leaning on my elbows, I kissed her deeply, dancing my tongue in her mouth.

"Levi... Levi..." Her jade-green eyes stared into mine. Her body shuddered all over, then her pussy clasped my cock as she moaned. I scooped my hips into her a few more times with the same relentless pace.

"Want you to do that again." I punched my hips harder, but still held her and kissed her.

She was out of breath. "I can't."

"Yes, you can, dollface. Come for me again." My dick could make her peak on command. I had discovered her spot and now knew which button to press. A few more pushes there, and she... yep, she came again.

"Please, Levi... Please. I can't."

"Shh, shh. I got you." My dick slipped out as I knelt, but entered her again, more forcefully. Increasing the intensity and pace of my thrusts, I held her legs up and open for me. I moved her foot to my face and sucked on her beautifully painted toe. Her back bowed, and she writhed on me with as much passion as I was humping her with.

My eyes held hers. I had never made love with anyone before. Pretty sure that's what this was. It was different; it was the best sex of my life. Probably too tacky to tell her while fucking her, though, so I'd say it later. The right moment. But I could show her with my body.

I pressed her button one more time so she would come, and as she did, I leaned forward to hold her scream in my mouth as I came with her. I kissed her as my whole body relaxed into hers. She threw her legs around my waist and strung her hands through my hair. I never wanted to leave this moment with her, but there was something I needed to do.

"Elle," I panted. "I want you to stay here, here in my bed, but there are some things I need to take care of. That sounds like how I left things before, in the Bahamas. But this time, you've set me free, and I'm stepping through the door you opened for me. I'm going to take care of us." I pulled her hand up to my mouth and kissed it. "Will you be here when I get back in a few hours?" She seemed unconvinced. "Okay, go home, and I'll come to you... if I can sneak in somehow."

"I'll stay. Your bed's comfortable." She smiled, and I kissed her. She rolled over and pulled the sheets up while I got dressed.

After getting dropped off at the neighborhood

gate, I walked up to my father's house. I was going to walk right through the front door and not sneak in through my bedroom window. Things were different now. I'd never felt so light; it was like starting life all over again.

I spied a car in the driveway that I didn't recognize, but I continued my journey. Heading to my room, I packed up all of my items in bags and suitcases. I knew where my father hid my phone, so I sneaked into his bedroom and found it in the drawer of his bedside table. I wanted to keep those memories Elle and I had made together. I sent the evening's video from the new phone to my email so I could add it to my collection.

Making my way to my father's office, I heard voices inside. I knocked and entered without waiting for a response. Warren and Samantha were engaged in a heated exchange. The two quieted as soon as I entered. "Son, where have you been?"

"What's going on?" I looked between the two of them. My father was standing on the opposite side of his desk, and Samantha was in front of the club chairs. They both seemed angry.

"I left my purse the other day at dinner and came back for it. I also wanted to speak with Warren about the way things were left between us," Samantha said with heat in her eyes directed at my father.

"Between you and me?" I asked.

"Samantha feels she is owed something for the

time you two shared." My father's expression screamed, "*See! I told you so!*" louder than any words could.

"Oh. Pay her and be done with it. Who cares?" Samantha scoffed.

I slammed my new phone down on his desk. "Here's your fucking phone back." I didn't care if this woman heard what I was about to say. "I'm married to Elle Townsend and I'm not annulling the marriage. I will have the best marriage of anyone in the Joseph family, a great marriage, one of legends."

He tried to interrupt me, but I continued, "I know about you, *John*. I know what you tried to do to her, to us. It's not going to work. You're not going to break us up. I'm not yours to control anymore. I will work harder at this marriage than anything in my life. I don't care if I'm never successful in my career. If I have her, I have everything."

He looked aghast, jaw wide open. Samantha was getting redder by the moment. I loved that I was saying this in front of a stranger. Warren's ego would explode due to embarrassment.

"Don't bother disowning me. I don't want a fucking dime from you. Goodbye, *Father*." I said the endearment like the joke it was.

Lawson was waiting for me outside the door. I asked if he'd take me to the TRZ house so I could be with my wife.

Warm arms wrapped around me in Levi's comfortable, warm bed. I snuggled back into him and turned my head as he kissed me. "Told you I'd be back." We cuddled and slept naked in each other's arms.

When I woke up, Levi was still there. His wild bed hair had me giggling until he peeked open an eye. "What?" His voice was morning husky.

"Your hair."

"Yeah, it gets bad. You better get used to it." He pulled me closer and planted a kiss on my temple.

I ran my fingers through his wavy locks, twirling them and scratching my fingernails on his scalp as he relaxed and moaned. "Levi, I never slept with anyone else while—I should never have reached out to John after the Bahamas. I just didn't have anyone to talk to." His eyes opened to watch me as I leaned over him.

"I didn't want to get the marriage annulled. I thought you did."

His light brown eyes sparkled in the morning light, a beam streaming through an open curtain. "I know. I didn't, either. I mean, I didn't have sex with anyone else, and I didn't want our marriage annulled; I didn't want to be apart from you. I wasn't the one to send those papers, it was my father." He ran his fingers through my hair. "His obsession with you, I can understand... but he won't be in our lives any longer."

I worried he had done something, like take an axe to his father last night. I asked suspiciously, "What did you do?"

Levi laughed. "I didn't kill him, surprisingly. I just took my stuff from his house and brought it here." He pulled my head into his chest. "I have enough crypto to pay for next semester's tuition, but that's about it."

He rolled on top of me, holding my arms down, and kissed my nose. "I don't have a phone," he smiled, "or a car. Or probably a way to pay for any food or take you on dates, yet. But I swear to you, Elle, I'll make you the happiest wife for the rest of our lives."

"And I'll make you the happiest husband." I kissed him, morning breath and all. "Levi, you won't just take care of me. I'll take care of you, too. We will take care of each other." He fell onto my body, head next to mine, and held me tightly.

"I love you, Elle. Told you, I always have."

I teared up and took a breath. "And I love you, Levi. Always have."

As he kissed me on the temple, he scooped his thickening erection into my stomach and wrapped his arms tightly around me as much as I wrapped myself around him. I scooted up so I could feel his hardness on my core. We humped each other that way, groaning and kissing until I was so wet that I was able to push up my hips and wiggle his hard cock inside.

"We should have a movie night," he said.

"O-okay." An odd thing to bring up. He felt so good, my brain was melting. His voice was so alluring, he could talk about the weather, and I think I'd still come.

"Watch our videos together." He raised one side of his lips in a smug grin.

I laughed. "Well, we need more shots. Grab your camera." I think Levi knew how sexy I felt while being filmed for him. I loved knowing he was watching these videos when I wasn't around and getting turned on.

"Fuck, dollface. Giggle again. That feels so good on my dick." I laughed, and his eyes almost rolled into the back of his head as he moaned. He sat up, remaining inside me, and reached over to grab his phone. "No service, but still useful." He hit the button to record a video from above me. When he plunged inside, my large tits bounced, and he grabbed one, groaning, "Fuck, hotness, right there."

I pushed my butt into the mattress, curving my hips to get him in deeper. He began panting harshly as I did. He moved one hand from the camera to palm my waist as he thrust. "I love putting my cum inside you, fucking you raw." Levi had found my magic spot and knew exactly how to push it to get me to come. "Cream all over my dick, dollface." My pussy clenched, and I writhed on the bed with my orgasm. "Mmm, that's a good girl, coming all over your daddy's cock."

Levi threw his phone down and grabbed my hips to control my body. He forcefully thrust into me, and I could feel myself getting ready to come again. As I felt his cock start to pulse within me, filling me with cum as he groaned, I came again.

He collapsed on the bed beside me and puffed out, "I don't know. Is morning sex with my wife the best? I'll have to compare it to afternoon and night sex. Be scientific about it."

I flipped over half on top and gave him a quick peck on the cheek. "I need to go home and shower. Probably should study sometime today."

He grabbed my waist with an arm and teased, "Nope. You need to leave my cum in there all day. I wanna feel it when I fuck you later."

"Ha. I will tonight; how about that? I'll sleep with it inside of me."

"Compromising. Already a perfect marriage." He sucked my lips into his. "I've got life stuff to take care of now that I'm broke. Markets aren't open for trading. I'll do that Monday; I hope to make some money. I need to figure out if I can still use my credit cards until my father shuts them off. Buy some basics before he does. Can I meet up with you later?"

"Absolutely. I'll make us dinner; I won't let my husband starve."

Before I could get up from the bed, he grabbed my arm. "Hey. I love you."

I smiled. "I love you, too."

"We should talk about you moving in here. I mean, on the down low. We're married. Married couples live together. Xavier won't care."

Pulling on my costume from his floor, I said, "not sure how I feel about living with a bunch of nasty frat guys." His sheet slid down his body as he sat up to watch me dress, exposing his chest. "But... I'll consider it." I didn't tell him, but I got butterflies in my stomach thinking about living with Levi, my husband. The TRZ manor wasn't my Barbie dream house, but it was close.

After making it home and cleaning myself up, I brought my oatmeal and coffee to my desk to start studying. Listening to gentle rain sounds through my headphones, I settled in, preparing for a long session. My stomach twisted into a knot when I received a notification that I had a chat message on the sugar baby website. I hadn't had a moment to delete the account yet.

I was going to do just that without even a glance at the message, knowing it was from Levi's father. However, it wasn't a chat message. John, or Warren, had sent me a video. I was in the thumbnail of the video. It was from last night. The video of me giving Levi a blowjob in the bathroom. If someone didn't know what I was wearing last night, they wouldn't know it was me. My sunglasses and pink wig hid enough of my face to make me unrecognizable.

Some chat messages started rolling in after the post:

> DaddyJ007: He released this all over the internet. Congratulations, whore, you're officially married to your pimp now.

> DaddyJ007: That boy holds grudges way too long. Guess he didn't handle us being together very well.

> DaddyJ007: I could have helped you, angel. You have never known what's best for you, and now I'm afraid you're facing the consequences. Will Townsend would be so disappointed.

Nausea flooded my guts. I ran into the bathroom and vomited. Was the video really all over the internet? I brushed my teeth and showered a second time, feeling incredibly dirty. Maybe no one would see it. Maybe no one would recognize me. Was Warren threatening me? Threatening to tell my father? Did my father see the video? Did Levi do this? Was this a trick?

Levi and I were too young to get married, especially so quickly. Perhaps he had been setting me up by filming me for sex; he knew I liked it. What if he had shown his friends our videos? What if he laughed and made fun of me while uploading them for everyone to see? I wondered if that was what he did while I was asleep in his bed last night.

Levi never changed from the person he was in elementary school. From the boy in Trent's basement. This was exactly the type of trick he would play. He *was* probably laughing with his friends right now. Maybe Levi even won some money for it. I could see Xavier's face with a smug grin calling me Smelly Ellie. All the old insecurities came flooding back, images of being shoved into the dirt as the boys laughed at me.

I was over the drama from this relationship. Levi and his father were trouble. Perhaps I should have listened to my mother all along. I needed a nice, rich man to take care of me. Maybe Warren was right, too. I didn't know what was good for me; I made horrible decisions and chose the wrong men.

After pacing around in a towel, I heard a small knock on my bedroom door. "Yeah?"

"Elle, are you okay?" It was Sharice. We didn't speak much; we were often busy, she with her music and me with a psychotic sugar daddy and pimp of a husband.

I went to the door and opened it. She hurried in and closed the door behind her. "Um... Have you checked your socials?"

Doom struck my body. I ran to grab my phone—notifications from about an hour before filled the home screen. The video had been uploaded, and I was tagged in it. Levi didn't have an account anymore, so he wasn't. You couldn't see him in it, just his large cock in my mouth.

"It'll get taken down pretty quickly. They don't allow porn... uh, these types of videos on the website," she said as tears filled my eyes. She rushed over and put her arms around me. I put my face into her neck and cried. I didn't care if we hadn't been close friends, we were now. She patted me on the back. "I already flagged the post." Her face pulled back to look into mine. "Who did this?"

"I'm... not sure."

"You don't have to tell me. But this looks like the pants Levi was wearing last night." She waited. "Did he do this?"

I hesitated, then nodded. Never again would I allow myself to be used by him for entertainment. Levi Joseph was a mean boy. And I wasn't going to let him kiss me ever again.

Sharice kindly offered to be my bodyguard. She wasn't going to allow Levi anywhere near me. She also wasn't going to tell anyone unless I said she could. I didn't want to hear the "I told you so's" from my family or the "he's such a player" from all my friends.

I spent the afternoon deleting my social media accounts and sugar baby accounts—basically scrubbing my online persona. I was majoring in business with an emphasis on public relations. What was I even doing if I couldn't fix my reputation?

The rest of the afternoon, I tried to focus on my studies, putting my headphones on for a distraction, but it wasn't working. I tried some yoga and meditation but couldn't concentrate.

Another knock came on my door. "Come in."

Sharice popped her head in. "Hey, girl. I'm ordering Thai food. Do you want some?"

"Yes! That's exactly what I need. I can't study right now." Sharice placed the order, and I lay on my bed, listening to music, trying to drown out my still-beating, wounded heart.

The food must have arrived. Sharice answered the door. I listened from my bedroom as Levi's voice bellowed from the hallway outside our apartment. "What do you mean, I can't see her?"

I couldn't hear Sharice's responses, just Levi's angry yelling. "What are you talking about? I didn't do anything. What video?" The door closed, and the deadbolt was drawn. Pounding could be heard throughout the apartment until my door rattled.

Kinsley came out of her room. "What is going on?"

Sharice looked at my door while I glimpsed out into the common area of the apartment. "Um... some drunk fraternity guy. He's at the wrong apartment but doesn't believe me."

"Elle!" Levi wailed between thuds. "Please, Elle! What's going on?! Elle!" He seemed to be crying. "Elle!"

"That doesn't sound like he's at the wrong apartment. Elle?"

I stepped out of my room. "Maybe we should call security." Kinsley nodded and grabbed her phone to dial the front desk and campus security.

Between wailing and crying and shouts of my name, the pounds continued another ten minutes before a few deep male voices seemed to instruct Levi to do something. Levi yelled back at them. There was a scuffle. I dared peek through the peephole where a delivery boy was standing with our food, his back pressed against the wall in fear. Levi thrashed against two large security officers, screaming my name as they dragged him away, one grabbing his arms and the other his legs.

I stepped back from the door and said, "Food's here!" Trying my best to seem like nothing happened. The girls picked up on it and opened the door for food, and we sat at the dining table. I twirled some noodles around my chopsticks and glanced at my roommates.

Kinsley met my gaze when I looked up. She said,

"So... was that Levi Joseph?"

"Um, yeah. I think so. Guy seems pretty unstable," I responded. "I think I'll finish this in my room. I have a ton of studying to do."

Sharice interrupted, "Elle, if you need to talk, we are here for you. Anytime."

"Thanks." I didn't need to talk anymore. I needed action. Stepping into my room, I set the box of noodles on my desk and did something I had never done before; I called my mother.

"Elle? Are you okay?" Veronica said in surprise.

"Yeah, Mom. Um... you and Emilia and Elizabeth were talking about some guys you wanted to set me up with? I think... I'm ready."

"Oh! Yes, we have lots of eligible bachelors! Let's see. Mitch Jenkins works for your father. He's forty-two but would love to settle down with someone younger. You'd be perfect. Or there's Jeremy Davis. Yes, he's only about thirty-five. He does something in tech, very wealthy. You can look past his nose."

"Anyone is fine. Just set us up. Let me know when."

"Honey, I am so proud of you. Better start taking those prenatal vitamins!"

I hung up.

I would get my revenge and lead a happy life... without Levi Joseph. Levi would never save me from anything; I was just a game to him. No more waiting around for someone to rescue me. I was going to save myself.

Things were dire. I had no money and a cheap phone with a pay-per-month service. I had to cash out crypto to buy a clunker of a car to make it to classes. Xavier offered to give me one of his extra vehicles, but I couldn't do that. I wanted to earn my way; no more handouts.

Elle blocked my new number as soon as I texted her, but not before responding:

MY WIFE

We got married too young. Sign the papers.

I had to borrow Xavier's phone the day I was accosted by campus security to see which "video" Elle's roommate had been talking about. It was the one I took from Halloween night. My father's work, no doubt. He couldn't stand the fact that I had won

178

his prize. He would never let me be happy without his controlling hand around my neck. I would kill him if I didn't want to stay out of prison; if I was locked up, I'd never get Elle back. I started to believe the only way I'd be free was if he were dead.

I tried to communicate with Elle in every way I could over the last few weeks. She wasn't reading my emails. Security had banned me from her building, and any time I went near, Mary or whoever was managing the front desk would threaten to call them. Once, I tried to throw pebbles at her window and yell that I didn't do anything and please talk to me and then just screamed her name, but Aaron and Brock came and took me away.

Yes, I was now on a first-name basis with my two campus security guards. If I played my cards right, I figured I could get an invite to Brock's kid's first birthday party. Free cake and probably food. Maybe they'd even have gift bags. Things were dire.

I tried to get to her through her friends and room-mates, but they wouldn't even take a piece of paper with a poem and explanation written on it to give to her. She stopped going out to Manny's and Tony's. I didn't see her at the club on Fridays. She didn't come around to the TRZ house.

I was starting to wonder if I should give up. How could she not understand that I loved her? I've never loved anyone or anything. How could she not know I wouldn't do something like release that fucking video? I didn't want anyone to see my wife naked, except for me.

Adam offered multiple ways to help me, including slipping sub sandwiches into my backpack when he met me on campus. I'd let him do that, but nothing more. I was done being a Joseph, and I certainly didn't want anything from them. There were strings attached to anything they offered that formed the noose I was trying to slip out of.

When I thought things couldn't get worse, Adam gave me the terrible news one Wednesday afternoon when he met me on campus. Our mother had planned her first trek to visit us for Thanksgiving. Adam was going to host her at his place and wanted me to meet his new girlfriend. I guess his new gal had encouraged him to try to reconnect with his mother. I already didn't like her, whomever she was.

"Yeah, I don't think I can make it," I said as he put a footlong sub in my bag and zipped it up.

"I'm catering it. Mashed potatoes, turkey, gravy, stuffing... pies... and that's plural, Levi."

I sighed. "Ugh. Being poor sucks. Fine. What time?"

Later that day, I was on the living room sofa at the manor, sipping a skunked beer someone left in the back of the fridge, eating my backpack footlong. Xavier walked in and sat beside me with some brown bags of food and groceries. He pulled out a deli sandwich from a bag and took a bite without looking at me.

"Still not talking to you, huh? I got it taken down everywhere I could."

"I know." I didn't want to talk about the video. It just made me sick. But I was grateful that Xavier used his contacts to eradicate the video as much as he could. "I mean, thanks." Xavier always knew how to handle problems. "I'm not sure it will make a difference at this point."

"I haven't seen her when I'm over there. I don't think she's *with* anyone."

I nodded. Xavier was dating Elle's best friend and roommate. Though, his girlfriend was at the manor more than at their apartment these days. "Does Marissa—"

"No, she doesn't mention anything." Xavier finished his sandwich in two bites. "Look, Lev. I'm not sure things are going to turn around. I know this thing between you two has been going on for a long time, but maybe... maybe it's time to move on."

Other than my family, no one knew. Xavier was the closest person to me. He was a vault. I could tell him. "I married her."

If Xavier ever actually felt the human emotion of shock, his face did a good job resembling it. Eyebrows slightly raised, he said, "Oh?"

"About two months ago. We stepped in for him and Whitney when Adam's wedding was supposed to take place. That picture on my social media? That wasn't fake. We weren't messing around. I married her. We're married. She's my wife."

Xavier swallowed and leaned back on the couch as if contemplating his next move. He sat forward again and put an arm around my shoulder. "Well, there's only one solution."

"Yeah?"

"You have to get her back." Whenever Xavier wanted something, he got it. He never let anything get in his way. It's why we were so competitive with each other during games. I admired his tenacity.

I smiled. He patted me on the back. "Congratulations, man."

"Thanks, but I'm not sure how to win her back when she won't even…"

Xavier got up and shoved the grocery bags toward me with one foot. "You should knock her up. That'll do it."

I snorted. That sounded more like his thing. "What's this?" I pointed to the bags of food.

"You got a mini-fridge. Use it." Xavier walked off before I could protest. I carried the bags to my room and put the food away in my closet and mini-fridge. At least I had snacks for the rest of the week or so.

When Thanksgiving Day rolled around, I drove to Adam's apartment. I was late, thanks to my crappy, always flat car tires. When I knocked, Caitlyn Watson answered the door.

"Oh, you have *got* to be fucking kidding me," I rolled my eyes. "Adam. Seriously?"

Caitlyn looked hurt but opened the door further and flipped her red hair over one shoulder. "Well, hello to you, too, Levi."

I marched into the dining area, where my mother sat. She had aged quite a bit, allowing gray hairs to penetrate her temples, and had stopped using Botox. She looked better but tired, gaunt instead of her usual fit thinness. Her brown eyes lit up when she saw me, "Levi!" She hurried to grasp me in her arms. I don't recall the last time a family member hugged me.

"Hello, Cindy." I pulled away, placing my coat on the back of a chair.

"Oh, don't *Cindy* me. I'm your mother."

I snorted. "Okay. Where's the food?" If I wasn't so broke and hungry, there was no way I would hang out with Caitlyn and Cindy.

Adam and Caitlyn brought out some hot dishes and set them on the table. "Just getting the rolls," Adam said and returned to the kitchen.

"Let me help." I jumped up to go into the kitchen, leaving his clinger and the woman that gave birth to us to talk in the dining room. As soon as we were alone, I yelled, "What are you thinking? Caitlyn Watson?!"

"Levi... do not start with me. Caitlyn's changed. She's had it rough."

"She's using you to try to make Xavier jealous. She knows she can't use me."

"I'm not talking about whom I'm dating with you anymore." Adam grabbed the rolls and started to walk toward the dining room.

"Why not? I was right about Whitney." Adam whipped his head back to look at me but held his tongue and kept going.

I sat down at the table and filled my plate with food. Fine, he didn't want to hear from me? I'd eat and be on my way. Hopefully, I could feign deafness and not have to listen to these whores speaking.

"Levi, tell me about school. Are you seeing anyone special?" My mother asked.

"It's fine and no." I shoved a roll into my mouth. The faster I ate, the quicker I'd be out of there.

Caitlyn snorted. "Oh, he's not seeing anyone *special*. Just someone I think we've *all* seen." She narrowed her eyes at me from across the table. I guess she'd seen the video. God, I hated this bitch.

Adam reached for her hand. "Mother, how is the cranberry sauce? I know you used to like the berries and not the jelly."

"Oh, everything is so wonderful. Haven't had a Thanksgiving like this in a while."

"What happened to Ted? Your kids?" I asked.

Adam looked down. My mother took a big drink of her red wine and answered, "Ted and I haven't been together in a long time."

"Oh. Divorced?"

"Yes, we divorced, and then I married Robert. But then we divorced, and I just broke up with Eddie." She observed my reaction. "Dating is hard."

I chewed slowly, staring straight ahead, which was difficult because Caitlyn was within my field of view. My jaw clicked when I moved it forward. I inhaled and said, "So you've had how many husbands now?"

Adam tried to interrupt, but my mother had a fire in her eyes when she answered, "I don't need judgment from my son."

"Oh? How many fucking kids do you have now, *mother*?" Cindy looked down at her plate and then took a drink of wine. She started to answer, but I continued, "Where are they all?"

"None of this would have happened had your father given me the alimony I deserved. I *earned* that money, especially raising *you*. Ted was a lowlife that didn't make anything, either. He has our children, in case you wanted to know." She calmed and said wistfully, "I had another two with Robert. Would you like to meet your other siblings?"

"They aren't my siblings." I got up, pushing my chair back with my legs. "And you're not a mother."

Pleadingly, she responded, "Levi, I heard you gave up your inheritance from your father. If we worked together, we could get it back from him." She was desperate to keep me there, glancing toward Adam, who continued looking down while Caitlyn

185

stroked his back as if she cared. "Adam says... Adam thinks your father could get us the money we deserve."

"*Ohh*, I see. You came back for money. You left Warren for a bigger dick, then, what? Kept trying to marry up the food chain until you were broke and spent?" I grabbed my coat. "Trying to pretend to be a family. The four of us never were. I've never had one, but I'm going to make one. I'm going to make the best one."

I grabbed the entire breadbasket and the turkey dish with gravy and started to leave, but paused to top my pile with a pie, then dashed out of the apartment. My mother treated marriage like a joke. My father treated it like a commodity. I wasn't going to do that. My life was going to be different. I would end this generational curse and focus on having an amazing marriage and a stable family.

That had to start by getting Elle back. I wasn't going to give up on her. What kind of husband would I be if I threw in the towel every time we faced a trial? Elle may not be rooting for us, but I would. One of us had to. This time it would be me. Even if I had to fight for us a hundred times, I would do it. She was worth it; *we* were worth it.

Elle probably thought I'd released the video because of what I did in middle school. I'd have to prove to her I wasn't that kid anymore, that I took our marriage seriously. I was going to take care of us. She was my reason for living now. It didn't matter that I hadn't grown up in a good family; I could create one.

I drove over to Elle's family home. When I approached the door, I could see her large family inside enjoying dinner, everyone sitting around the table. Checking my outfit, I smoothed my zippered pullover under my pea coat and brushed crumbs from my jeans. Running a hand through my hair, I knocked on the door.

Yes, Mr. Townsend got up to check. He was exactly whom I wanted to see. As he neared, my heart raced. I'd never been nervous about speaking with him until now.

"Levi Joseph?" William Townsend appeared confused, but stood back to hold the door open. "Hey, son. Come in. What can I do for you?"

I sneaked in the front door and lowered my voice. "Um, actually, I wanted to see you. Is there somewhere..." I looked around his beautiful house. "Is there somewhere we can go where Elle won't see? I don't think she wants me here."

Will's face showed he already knew that his daughter had banned me from her presence. I thought he might kick me out, but he looked up and said, "Follow me."

I trailed him down a hall into an office with a pool table and bar. There were several TVs and a huge deer head on the wall. Movie theatre chairs surrounded the screens, all playing football games; it reminded me that Xavier, Big G, Mason, and I used to get together after eating to smoke up and watch football. Now that Xavier was occupied with Marissa and, I suspected, G was occupied with someone, our tradition had been broken. And I was glad about it if it meant I got Elle.

"Nice man cave, Mr. Townsend."

"Oh, please call me Will. You always have; no need for formalities." He walked to the office area. "Yeah, the place is nice. I have to have it… three daughters." He smiled and pointed to a couple of comfy chairs surrounding his desk. "What's going on?"

"How much do you know about Elle and me?"

He inhaled as if he knew this was exactly the question I would ask. Then, he spoke. "I know you love her. I can see it all over your face." I felt embarrassed, but he continued, "And she loves you."

"Yes, sir. It's true. I married her."

He was taken aback. Clearly, Elle had not told him. "Oh? When did—?"

"The Bahamas. I'm sorry how we went about it, but I'm not sorry I married her. She's the love of my life, and I'm going to take care of her. I told you I would." I wasn't sure how to explain everything to him. "She thinks I did something horrible that I didn't do. She won't talk with me and wants an annulment, but I won't let that happen. I'm not ever going to let that happen." My face must have let him know I meant business.

Will nodded soberly. Then, he broke into a big

smile. "Good." He came around and stuck out his hand for me to take, and I went to shake it, but he pulled me up into a hug. "Welcome to the family, son."

I could have cried. It was strange, and I wasn't sure how to take the gesture. But I had an ally, and that's all I needed.

Will got a mischievous grin. He poured two whiskeys from the bar, handed me a glass, and sat beside me in the other club chair. "I gotta tell you, Levi. You've got competition. Veronica has been setting her up with this tool named Brandon. I don't like the kid, which is probably why my wife did it."

I swallowed the vomit I felt coming up. Elle was dating someone? "How... When?"

Will put his hand on my shoulder and shook his head. "She doesn't like him. Don't worry. There's only one guy that's been on her mind ever since you guys were little." He clapped me on the back. "So, what was your plan?"

Feeling relieved that this douche Brandon may not have a chance, I spoke, "Well, two things I came to see you about, sir."

Will kicked his feet up on the desk. "Go on... this should be good."

"First, I'd like to ask you for a job. I mean, when I graduate... If I graduate. I am currently short on funds but hope some of my trades pay off to pay for my tuition."

"So, things with your father? I take it something happened."

I looked down and took a drink. "Yes, sir. He's no longer supporting me. Didn't agree with the marriage." *And he was trying to fuck your daughter.* I figured if Will knew that, I was sure he'd pick me over Warren.

"No question. I'm paying your tuition, and you most definitely are working for me." I gazed at him with shock. I didn't expect that. I thought I might have to jump through some hoops for that offer, but he just laid it out for me.

Sensing my disbelief, Will said, "You think I'd let Levi Joseph get away from my company and work for Cardell? You think I'd let my son-in-law work for someone else? Nope. You can pay me back by bringing in that crypto trade. I'll fund your MBA, too, if you want. You want a company car? You got it."

I smiled.

Will and I were kindred spirits. I could feel it. "What's the second thing?" he asked.

"I want you to teach me how to fish."

So glad I brought my tuxedo from my father's house to the manor when I moved. I needed it for the Cardell's Christmas party. I knew Elle would be there with her date, and I planned to lay things out there for her to understand.

Will was my new silent partner and informed me of Elle's whereabouts and happenings over the last few weeks. He also taught me about fishing whenever we could sneak away on his new boat (Apparently, winter fishing *in* the water is uncomfortable.) Not only had I learned a new fun hobby, but I'd also lured a new friend.

Did I want to go into the party knowing Elle was with some date and kick the shit out of him? Absolutely. But I had a better plan. One that wouldn't embarrass her to death and one that would definitely win her back. Okay, maybe. Maybe not today, but soon. At the very least, I hoped she'd hear me out and wouldn't eat my eyeballs out of my skull when she saw me.

The Cardells hosted the most ostentatious occasions. Millie Cardell was an event planner, and the holiday party was the highlight of the country club's year. Everyone ended up rocked by the end of the night. There would be gossip to last the ladies for months after. I planned to stay sober; I had avoided alcohol since I made my plan.

The Cardells stood at the end of the room with a crowd of people surrounding them. I greeted them respectfully. Growing up, Malcolm Cardell was the father I wanted. I would pretend I was a part of Xavier's family whenever I was invited on their vacations or over to dinners. Xavier's sister died when we were young, then his mother when we were in high school. It was a rough time for him, but George, Mason, and I helped him get through it. Mal married Millie a few years ago, and the two became the town's royal couple.

I nodded at Will Townsend and ignored Veronica, who was flirting with some councilperson while Will stood beside her. Elle's sisters and their husbands were in attendance, looking demure and pretentious. One of her sisters (I didn't know which) was already pregnant. Veronica would be thrilled about that. *Wait until I put a baby in Elle*, I thought while smirking at my mother-in-law.

My father was there with Samantha. I wondered if she had blackmailed him into being his date to snag an invite to the year's most prestigious event. She was probably going to try and trade up while here. Gals like her were usually looking for who had the deepest pockets, just like my mother.

My game face on, I waited for my wife to arrive with her date. As she waltzed in, I coughed in shock at her beauty. She wore a bright red gown with a heart-shaped neckline displaying her generous cleavage. The sleeves were made of patterned lace, and the full skirt ended at her shins. She wore tall red peep-toe heels and red lipstick. It should have been me there next to her, holding her arm instead of that penis with hair.

The party was held in a large white tent set in the backyard of the Cardell estate. As Elle and her date stood near the entry, I strolled up and stuck my hand out to the penis to introduce myself. "Hello, I'm Levi Joseph. I see you brought my wife to this event." From this distance, I could already smell her mango scent.

Brandon sputtered, not raising his hand, and looked at Elle, who said, "Don't be rude, Levi. Please leave us alone."

"I'm sorry. What is going on?" Penis spoke. He had a whiny voice and an ill-fitted tuxedo. I could see why Will didn't like him.

"You brought my wife as a date to this event. I'll be

watching you closely." I sauntered to a nearby drink station and tuned my ears to the aftermath.

Her date immediately started to impale her with questions. That was not a good sign; it meant he was into her and cared if she was already taken and not there just for a good time. Elle put him off by saying she "married him too young" and that things were not working out. Not working out my ass.

Maybe I should get drunk.

I'd have one drink to cool my nerves.

The crowd was called to attention for dinner. We all moved to take our seats; Elle and penis headed to the same assigned table as me. I felt a bit hazy from my drink; I'd been sober for so long that my tolerance was quite low. It would give me the confidence I needed to get my wife back.

Before I could sit, Xavier waltzed to the dance floor and proposed to his girlfriend, Marissa. It was a welcome distraction. The two had only been together a few months, but when Xavier made up his mind about something, he didn't change it. I got up to congratulate them with our friends.

Elle came over with her date, and I made a pointed comment that Xavier and Marissa were "way too young" to get married. Elle scoffed, appearing offended.

Well, dollface, you'd said it.

When we returned to our table to eat, Elle and Brandon sat in their assigned seats next to me. Elle sat between me and the penis with her back to me. Brandon had her body between his legs. He looked like he was way too old for her. I felt the urge to pummel him when he scooted closer to her body. Fury radiated from me. He tried to whisper to her, but she looked over at me.

I could get a second drink.

This was not going how I thought it would go.

Brandon said softly to her, "Do you need another drink?"

I snorted, "Trying to get her plastered? Is that how a face like yours has to resort to getting girls?"

Elle snapped her neck to me and mouthed, "Stop it."

Brandon's eyebrows raised, then he pursed his lips. "We're having a private conversation here."

"It's impressive how you can fit your entire vocabulary into one sentence, my man." I sipped my drink.

Elle said, "Ignore him. I do."

Brandon laughed.

"Yeah, and her pussy will have to ignore how small your dick is in order to orgasm."

At the same time, both of them yelled at me words I couldn't exactly make out.

"Elle. I need to talk with you privately," I said politely, using my smile.

"No."

I gasped. "I just need to speak with you for a minute."

"I said no, Levi."

"Take the hint. She's not into you," Brandon said.

That was it. I stood and grabbed him by the collar, but Elle squeezed between us before I could. "Stop it. I'm not talking with you. Sign the papers. I'm done with you." She grabbed her purse and left the tent, heading towards the house and restrooms.

Instead of following her, I took a break and grabbed a second drink. I shouldn't kill Brandon. It wouldn't look good for my chances of getting her back.

I wandered over and chatted with Xavier and Marissa. I talked with Mason, and Big G. Spoke to some of the TRZ guys. None of the distractions were working. Neither was my plan so far.

While contemplating a third drink, Will came over and clasped a hand on my shoulder. He said, "Son, you're all right. You're okay. You got this. That kid doesn't stand a chance. Don't sweat it. Look," he pointed to her table where the penis sat alone, "she hasn't even been with him half the night."

I looked back to our table and noticed he was right. Elle had been gone a long while. Brandon was looking around the tent the same as I was. "Yeah, I should go find her." I set my drink down and went toward the house.

I was familiar with the Cardell's place from my childhood days and nights here. Fun memories flooded my mind with each room I entered. After searching downstairs and clearing the bathrooms, I started to explore outside—still, no Elle.

Rounding a corner of the gardens, I heard arguing. On closer inspection of the darkened alley between the hedges, I saw my father pushing Elle up against the wall and trying to kiss her. She was thrashing and trying to push him off. Screaming, she shoved him, but he was forceful. I felt my body moving at lightning speed to grab him by the neck and throw him off her.

"You asshole! You stay away from her!" He started getting closer to me, so I jumped on him. I took him to the ground, and let my fists fly. Punch after punch landed on his face. Unformed words and obscenities emerged from my mouth while blood splattered around my fists.

My father started laughing while I was beating him, which only made me more enraged. I grabbed him by the collar, lifting his upper body off the ground while I straddled him. He looked at my wife, spitting out, "Elle, do you see? He's trying to be heroic, but you know what he did." The grip I had on his throat strangled his voice.

Samantha came around the corner, her tight V-neck sequined gown leaving little to the imagination. She gasped and ran towards us when she spotted me on top of Warren. "What is going on?!" She tried to tug back on my arm, but I wasn't letting go.

Ignoring her, I turned back to the man who tried to kiss my wife. "What do you mean? What did *I* do?"

"You made her a whore, exposing your sick videos like that to everyone," he said, leaking blood from his mouth.

"I did no such thing." Flipping my head to look at Elle while holding my father's neck, I said, "Elle, I never would do that. I understand why you'd think I would, but I didn't. I love you."

"*Sure*, you didn't." My father continued to speak.

"She's a whore. I bet she did it herself." Samantha was throwing daggers with her eyes at Elle. She was still trying to break my father and me apart.

"What? No, I didn't! Who are you, lady?" Elle exclaimed.

I didn't think my father was lying. Perhaps he didn't release the video. "If you didn't, who posted it?" As I asked the question, I realized... that night, I had slammed the phone on his desk. The woman who had been angry with how I'd left things, who wanted more money from my father, who wanted a relationship with me—Samantha.

"Samantha." I dropped Warren and got up. Samantha backed up on her heels. "*You*. You did this." I crept closer to her.

"What? Why would I?" Samantha shook her head, eyes wide, trying to look behind her at where she was walking.

"Because you're pissed off at the way I left things, figured you'd get back at me, break Elle and me up." I was pointing my finger in her face. She could go no further without plummeting into the hedges.

"She's a whore. Why can't the Joseph men see this? I needed you *both* to understand that. Everyone should see what a fucking slut she is." She dragged her fingers down my arm and fluttered her lashes at me. "Levi, she can't give you what you need. Not like me. We had a good thing going."

Removing her hand from my sleeve, I said, "So you admit it."

"Yes, I did it. And I'll remove it... for a price." She looked between the three of us.

I stood my ground. "You and my father deserve each other."

My father struggled to stand. I ran back to Elle. I grasped both her hands, and she let me. "Elle, I love you. I would never do something like that. I was a child when I showed off that makeout video. You're mine now. I never want anyone else to see you except for me. Do you believe me now?"

She nodded with tears in her eyes but yanked her hands from mine and quickly moved toward the front of the house.

I hurried to catch her. "Hey, can I take you home?"

"Please, Levi. Get me out of here." She didn't even turn to mumble to me.

"Okay, I got you." I snagged her by the waist protectively. "Do you need your purse? You got everything?"

"Oh, I forgot it." She stopped, a hand flying to her forehead.

"I can run and grab it or tell Marissa to make sure she grabs it for you."

Elle contemplated her answer but spoke, "Will you please run and get it for me?"

I kissed her on the forehead and rushed back to the tent. Working through the crowd on the way back to our table, I saw Brandon still sitting alone. Fucker hadn't even tried to find his date. When I grabbed my wife's purse from the table, he started to object, but I said, "I'm taking my wife home. *With me.* Lose her number. She's taken." I picked up my peacoat and Elle's fuzzy white cloak from the back of our chairs.

Brandon huffed, "I'm not into that polyamory thing, anyway. Too complicated. I'm out." He downed his glass of whiskey, threw his napkin on the table, and stomped out the backdoor. I darted out the side entrance and back to Elle.

The rented snow machines were blowing over the driveway as she stood underneath an arc of icy glitter lit only by moonlight, and twinkling white lights hung in nearby trees. Her hair glowed when she twirled, jittery with the sound of my footsteps approaching. "It's me," I called out to ease her anxiety.

"Oh, thank you, Levi."

"I had to park down the road because of all the cars." Standing behind her, I slipped her cloak over her shoulders as she took her purse. I put on my coat and threaded my fingers through hers, holding hands on our way to my car. "Are you okay, Elle?"

"I think I will be?" She looked grim. "I should have trusted you."

"Meh, I did some stupid things as a kid. Well, also, as an adult. I don't blame you." I squeezed her hand tighter.

"I do. I was so concerned about making the wrong decisions because I was never allowed to make any. I thought someone else should make them for me. When I was faced with one, I screwed it up. Instead of going to you, listening to you, I assumed the worst."

We reached my beater, and I walked her to the passenger door. She turned her back on it to face me. "I'm sorry, Levi. I'm so sorry. You didn't give up on us, and I did." She placed her cold palm on my cheek, and I covered it with my warm hand.

"I love you. I'm not going to give up on us, *ever*. No matter how much you try to push me away, I will fight for our marriage." I bit my lip, not knowing if I should ask the next question or what I would do with her answer. "Did you sleep with him?"

"Who? Your father?!" She looked disgusted.

"No, Brandon. Or... anyone. Or my father." *Fuck*, I didn't want to know that answer.

She laughed. "No. Definitely not. With anyone. I wouldn't. Not while—"

"While we're married," I finished for her.

She nodded. "I love you, Levi."

Unable to contain myself any longer, I grasped her head and devoured her mouth. She moaned inside of mine. I kissed down her neck and shoved my knee between her legs, parting her pretty red dress. Elle began humping me while panting sweet little breaths in my ear. I sucked and bit hard on her collarbone and up her neck, marking her. "Dollface, I need you. I have to be inside you. I have to come inside you. Please."

"Levi," she said, pulling me by my hair to look at her. She sucked my lips into hers, but again dragged herself back from me. "I, I need time."

All I could think of was time to get her back to TRZ and fuck the shit out of her until she got that brain-dead look again. "Hmm? Time?"

She panted as I suckled down her cleavage. "Levi." She started humping again, then stopped. "I want you. But I need some time." I stopped and stood back, arms pressed on either side of her, blocking her into the car. I was confused.

Elle shivered and said, "I want to make my own decisions and make them good ones. We fell into this marriage thing way too fast." I started to feel a sting of pain when she quickly said, "I don't regret it. I mean, I only got to date you for less than twenty-four hours beforehand. I don't know what our future looks like. You're so passionate and rash that sometimes I'm afraid I was just an excuse for you to irritate your father. And maybe I was using you to aggravate my mother."

"*Was* I an excuse for you? You certainly weren't for me."

"No. I don't know. If I jump into bed with you right now, right away, I won't make good decisions. Your penis has a way of making me incapable of thought." I smirked and started to growl at her, but she held me back. "Levi, I'd like time. I want to date you."

I pulled her back from the car and opened the door, situating her inside. I leaned over her, snapped on her seat belt, and looked her in the face.

"You want to date your husband? I'm going to date you so hard you won't even know what year it is."

fourteen

ELLE

After the Cardell's party, Levi dropped me at my apartment, but not before escorting me to the door and placing a chaste kiss on my cheek, telling me I was the most beautiful woman in the world. Before getting into his old rusted car, he yelled, "Unblock my number!"

This serious dating thing was new to me. Brandon took me out a few times, but he was tedious. I tried to avoid being alone with him. I thought it would be easy to go out with him because my mother approved. I wasn't attracted to him at all, so no fear of falling into bed with him. Instead, every conversation and event with him had been torturous. I planned to be polite, thank him for escorting me to the party, and then break things off first thing in the morning.

The next day, I unblocked Levi's number and removed the email filter that sent his messages to my trash. The ones not deleted, I read his desperation to contact me. I felt guilty about cutting him off and not giving him a chance to explain. Even though I hadn't known Warren Joseph was my sugar daddy, I was embarrassed that maybe Levi was secretly too disgusted with me. Maybe he wouldn't truly want me.

My mind kept thinking of my husband throughout the morning, despite trying to distract myself with anything but him. I didn't want to feel disappointed if he gave up on me, but I kept checking my phone to see if he'd texted.

It was winter break from school. My roommates were gone. Marissa and Kinsley were off with their boyfriends, and Sharice was back at her family's home. I didn't want to see my mother or sisters more than I had to.

I contemplated texting Levi to tell him I didn't need any more time, that I just wanted to be with him, but my phone rang. Jumping to answer it, I was disappointed when I saw who it was.

"Hello, Mother."

"Eleanor. You left poor Brandon alone at the party all evening. I take the effort of setting you up with a Watson of Watson cosmetics, and you squander his affections to run off by yourself? Maybe you need to go back to your etiquette classes. Do I need to pay for the course again?"

"I'm sorry, mother. I will call him to apologize." I

started pacing, wondering how I would get out of the conversation.

"Well, that is over now. His father personally called me to express their displeasure with your behavior. Nevertheless, I have a prospect. Not many are left, especially once the Watsons tell everyone how you acted at the party. It's slim pickings at this point."

"Mother, I don't need—"

She interrupted. "Warren Joseph approached your father and me last night talking about you. I think he is very interested in dating someone younger if—"

"—No. Absolutely not." My stomach rolled. "I will let you know when I'm ready to date someone else."

"But the New Year's party—," my mother whined.

"I'll let you know." I hung up and heard a knock on the front door. Through the peephole, I saw a delivery woman there. When I opened the door, she handed me a big brown bag. I said thanks while checking the tag on the outside. My name was written on it.

I set it on the dining table and peered inside. The sack contained waffles, pancakes, eggs, bacon, a bowl of fruit, and some sausage links. A handwritten note was at the bottom that said,

Morning meals aplenty
Never eating alone
I'll die before I'm thirty
If you don't answer your phone

Just as I read the note, my phone rang. It was Levi.

"Hi!" I answered excitedly.

"Dollface, I hope you enjoy your breakfast."

"This is so much food, Levi! I need help eating it all. You didn't have to spend the money on this." I didn't want to embarrass him but said, "I know it's tough for you right now."

"What's tough is not being with you," he paused. There was another knock on the door, and I went to it. Levi stood with his phone to his ear. "Can I join you for breakfast?"

My husband's presence always made me hyper-aware of every sensation. His stubble had been shaved for the party last night, and his wavy hair was perfectly styled, though a bit wet, as if he just had a shower. He wore a waffled cream-colored crewneck sweater with brown patches on the shoulders, black jeans, and camel brown boots. He smelled of amber with a hint of citrus.

Feeling self-conscious in my leggings and an over-sized sweatshirt, I opened the door further for him. I couldn't help but smile brightly and start sweating at the sight of him. I grabbed utensils while he spread the food for us on the table.

"I was hoping to take you out tonight if you're free." Levi shovelled almost an entire pancake in his mouth. He must be starving.

"Yes! Where are we going?"

"Have you ever been ice skating? The Cardells still have their pool ice rink set up from last night, and I asked if we could use it."

"Yeah, I'd like that."

We finished breakfast while he made me laugh about guests at the Cardell's party. He asked how I handled my mother today, knowing she was upset about leaving Brandon. I vented about her constant control. If there was anyone who would understand, it was Levi. "I'm envious you cut your father out of your life."

He smiled. "Feel free to walk through the cage door any time. It's open. I'll be waiting outside of it." Levi stood and helped to clean up from breakfast. Grabbing my hand, he led me to the front door. "I'll pick you up at 8?"

I nodded. "Okay." I was looking forward to kissing him again. Facing me, his scent enveloped me, and I began to tremble internally; I needed his penis. Levi's jaw was firm as he lifted a hand to cup mine. Ever so slowly, he placed his lips next to mine and sucked slightly, leaving with a slight lick of the tip of his tongue. I almost moaned.

"You had some syrup there." He pulled back and released my face, and smiled. "See you."

I almost fell over. My panties were wet. No kiss? That was it? Maybe I shouldn't have told him I needed time. I didn't, did I?

When he picked me up for our date, he slipped off the glove from my hand to hold it skin to skin. I was wearing Whitney's wedding band and noticed he had never removed his brother's ring. Levi watched me and twirled the band around my finger. "It's loose. Maybe we should get it sized if you like it."

"Yeah. Maybe. Yours fits well."

He nodded seriously. "Yeah, it's not coming off."

Leading me to the Cardell's backyard, he pulled off a backpack he had brought and set it down near the pool-turned-skating rink. Candy cane lights surrounded the outside, lighting up the beautiful white surface. It was so dark all the stars could be seen, twinkling lights interrupted by stretched cotton clouds casting a hazy glaze over the winter night sky.

"Have you ever done this before?" I asked him.

Levi laughed, "No, have you?"

"No! I guess we could fall with each other."

"I've already fallen for you." Levi smiled at me with his golden eyes. "They still had the skates from last night in the box to return to the rental company. Millie said she'd set some out for us. I wasn't sure what your size was." We found the boxes and put on skates. Mine were slightly too small, but they would work.

Levi turned on holiday music on his phone to set the mood, and we skated, hand in hand, laughing about our mutual incoordination. After probably several bruises, he asked if I needed a break. Returning to the bench outside the rink, I took off my skates to put my boots on while he dug out a thermos of hot chocolate and two mugs.

"These look like my father's camping mugs. He has these exact ones," I noted. Levi put an arm around me and lightly kissed my temple before sipping his drink.

"I've always loved your innocence. I felt angry most of my life, ready to rebel at any hint of disagreement. You give people the benefit of the doubt. I admire that. I need that."

"Well, I give people the benefit of the doubt, except for you with the annulment papers and the video," I said sadly. I wasn't sure if I could forgive myself for that.

Tucking me in further, he put my head against his shoulder. "You had good reason for thinking I'd done both of those things. Besides, it just let me know how much you cared. You wouldn't have been so angry with me if you didn't."

I turned my head to kiss him and sucked hot chocolate from his bottom lip. He moaned and slid his tongue tip across my lips. Setting our cups down, we grasped each other's faces, his hands threading through my hair and mine wrapped around his neck. I twisted to sit on his lap, facing him on the bench, and my nub was immediately aligned with his hardened erection contained by his black jeans. He held my thighs, pulling me even closer to his crotch. I ground on him, giving him a private lap dance. His coat covered my body, containing the heat we began to generate.

Levi stood and dropped me to my feet. "I think it's time to take you home."

"Wha—?" I felt chilled all over with his lack of warmth.

"I don't sleep around on the first date." He smirked so much I wanted to smack him.

"You're serious?"

He gathered our items and threw his backpack over his shoulder. Holding his hand out to me, he said, "Let's go."

I remained silent and contemplative on the ride to my place. Levi seemed in great spirits, bopping to every radio tune that came through his shitty speakers. Was it possible to get a blue clit? Like blue balls, but for girls? Before he could open my door, I was out and walking quickly to the front entrance. Levi ran behind me, chuckling. "Dollface, wait up."

I whipped around to him. "Are you coming up?"

He laughed, then slammed his mouth closed as if

to stop himself. "No. I will call you tomorrow, though."

I stomped inside, straight to my purple dildo, and tried to remember Levi's thick cock as I got myself off. Three times. Then fell asleep unsatisfied.

The rest of the week, Levi continued this pattern. He'd send me some type of delivery in the mornings, call or come over for brunch or lunch, then meet me somewhere for dinner or later.

The day after our ice skating adventure, he showed up with a large winter bouquet and oatmeal he'd made. He took me to the lounge for a live show that evening. We went bowling and grabbed hotdogs on another day. One night we sat by the fire pit at the Theta Rho Zeta manor and roasted marshmallows before watching a movie in their theater room. Levi took us to a fancy restaurant once, but I *insisted* upon paying. He'd already spent enough money that he didn't have.

Each evening was the same. We would make out, teenage style, until I couldn't stand it any longer, and he would stop us and take me home. My purple dildo was starting to become mundane. I begged him that I'd had enough time and was ready to be together, ready to start our marriage, and that I'd made a choice. He was it for me. I knew it. I'd always known it.

Each evening before we parted, Levi would tell me the reasons he loved me. He wrote me romantic and funny poems. He took pictures of us together on our dates "for our grandchildren." As he did, I was reminded why I had fallen in love with him.

Levi was assertive, something I lacked and respected. He was passionate about everything he did. His work ethic was commendable, especially since he had applied it to our relationship. I never had to fear a failed marriage if he were working this hard for us. I wanted to show him how much work I was willing to put in, too.

When I visited my parent's house Saturday morning to go fishing with Dad, I decided it was time for me to do what I had wanted for a long time. I was going to walk through the cage door. Levi would be on the other side, but, more importantly, I would be free.

My mother was in the kitchen talking with Elizabeth, who had announced her pregnancy at our Thanksgiving dinner. "Oh good, you're here. Dr. Forsythe is willing to take you out. He's less picky since he has those kids. I don't think he minds your *reputation*."

"It'll be a good opportunity for you, Eleanor, since Barry is no longer available," my sister said.

"I'm glad you're both here. I wanted to tell you that I'm not interested in dating anyone you set me up with because I'm already married." They both gasped, and I thought my mother might faint, but my father walked in and put a hand on her shoulder to calm her. He must have heard me from the hall.

"What do you mean *you're married*?!" My mother was hyperventilating at the same time my sister yelled, "Elle, what have you done?"

"Yes, I married Levi Joseph a few months ago in the Bahamas. We're in love. I love him."

The tizzy of words that ejected from their mouths made my father and I cackle loudly. I caught such phrases as "stupid childhood crush," and "he's a male whore" and "disowned," and "broke" (the last spoken by my mother with a hand to her mouth, face stricken in horror).

"I love Levi. My childhood crush grew up, and now he's a good man that treats me like a prize, so I don't care if we're broke. We will make our way. We will care for each other. So, I expect you all to treat him with the respect he deserves. He will be coming to family functions, and you will treat him like the family he is. He's my husband."

My mother and sister had never heard me speak back to them so emphatically. They were speechless for once in their lives. My mother turned to Dad to see his reaction as if to tell him to talk sense into me.

"I'm proud of you, sweetheart. I love Levi, too. And you're not going to be broke. He's joining Townsend Financial after graduation. He's also getting his MBA as part of our new employee education program." He was gripping my mother's shoulders.

"William!" Veronica was heated.

"I want our daughter to be happy, and I'm sure you do, too, Veronica. We welcome him to our family, don't we?" I'd never heard him talk to her that way.

She quieted at the sternness in my father's voice. "Yes. We do. Does Levi want children?"

I laughed. "I'll let you know when *we* decide if or when we want children."

"Let's go fishing!" My dad leaned down and kissed my stunned mother on her lips and hugged my sister before we headed out to the garage. "You haven't been in my boat yet."

"No, I'm nervous. You'll have to show me how to drive it. I brought extra hand warmers."

"Oh, it's stocked with stuff to keep us toasty. We should be good." Dad had packed the bed of his truck with supplies for the morning's outing. I'd told Levi I was out with my father on Saturday mornings fishing, so we would have to meet later.

"Dad, when did you talk with Levi?"

My dad peered straight at the road as he drove. "Oh, a few months ago. He's a good man. I always thought you two would end up together. I just worried about Warren interfering."

I swallowed. If only he knew. He looked at me out of the corner of my eyes, and I became suspicious that he knew something else. "Yeah. But Levi cut his father out of his life."

Dad cleared his throat. "Warren Joseph

approached me last winter. He was interested in you. And not for his sons."

My face flushed scarlet. "Oh?" I feigned innocence.

"I told him you were interested in a different Joseph and hoped he wished you two well... Don't think that turned out as I hoped."

"No, I don't think so."

Dad nodded and patted my thigh. "Sometimes it's better to have the family we create instead of the one we're given. Levi's got a father in me."

I teared up. "Thanks, Dad. I'm glad I was given you." I squeezed his hand.

Climbing down from his truck, I noticed a boat sitting at the dock with someone already inside it. I glanced at my father, who smiled. He handed me a cooler and some blankets and walked down with me toward the water.

Levi was standing still as a statue with a bright smile on his face. "What are you doing here?" I asked him.

"I'm taking you fishing." He held out his hand for me so I could get in the boat, and my father passed me the supplies from the dock.

"You two have fun," Dad said before waving goodbye.

L evi arranged the cooler and tackle boxes, securing them behind the seats. Dressed in his puffy vest over layers of plaid shirts and sweaters, he looked the part of a fisherman with a navy knit cap and orange waders with suspenders. He moved to the rear to start the engine near the rudder. "Take a seat, dollface. Let's go."

"Do you know how to drive this?" I didn't know Levi could pilot a boat like this and I was too nervous to ride with him.

He laughed. "Yes, I do. Sit down and put on your lifejacket."

I did as he instructed, and we darted through the whipping winter winds and snaking side waters. I pulled my hat down further over my ears and my scarf tighter around my neck. Levi seemed to know all the coves and found a calm pool of water under some overhanging trees. "We'll try here but may have to go to the deep part of the lake."

As he threaded his lines and prepared the bait, knowing exactly which tackle he wanted to use, I was stunned at his expertise. "When did you learn to fish?"

"I've been a few times... with Dad."

"Warren took you fishing?" I was confused.

"No, Dad. Will. Your dad. Our dad." He smiled gently as he sat and cast underneath the treeline.

"Huh. You and my dad have gone fishing together? How many times have you guys gone?"

"Just over the last several weeks." At my expression, Levi started dying laughing. "Stop making me laugh; you'll scare the bass away."

"You call him 'Dad'?"

"He asked me to. Believe me, your dad is much more of a father to me than mine ever was." He settled into his seat and waited. My father did always want a son. It made sense to me that my father and Levi would be good friends. How had I not seen it before? I was surprised they kept their relationship a secret from me.

My sister's husbands were too uppity for my dad. Even during the holidays, he often had to sneak away to be alone. Other than me, he had never taken anyone to his sacred fishing spots. Levi must mean a lot to him, which meant a lot to me.

Levi taught me how to winter fish since I had

never been before, wrapping his arms around me to hold the fishing line like I'd never used one. I pretended I hadn't so that I could be close to him. He showed me which bait was useful and which holes we should try, explaining how most fish dive deep to stay warm.

After trawling the first spot with no luck, he took us to the deepest part of the lake. I'd had enough fishing by then, so I wrapped myself in a blanket and shoved more hand warmers in my gloves. I watched my husband's handsome profile while he fished. I wondered if it was possible to have sex in a little boat without tipping over.

"You've done so much for us this week."

Levi glanced at me and asked, "What do you mean?"

"I mean, you've done this dating thing full speed. I'm impressed. I've enjoyed it. I like dating you."

"Well, it's not going to end. This is it. This is us now. We date." He was not having any luck with a catch, but he never seemed impatient. "I'm enjoying being out here with you."

"Me, too. I've enjoyed everything... Who knew little Levi Joseph would grow up to be so romantic." I opened the thermos he had of hot coffee. The sips helped to warm my insides.

"I thought marrying you at school was pretty romantic."

As Levi cast his rod again, I stopped my teeth chattering long enough to get out, "I've been begging you, Levi, but I'm serious. I've had enough time. I'm ready to do this. It was stupid to even ask to just date 'cause all I've done is punish myself by feening for you." He laughed and pulled his line in, putting our poles away.

Seeing how cold I was, he decided to take us in. Wrapping me in another one of my father's blankets, he started the engine and steered us back to the dock. After helping me out of the boat, he ran to his car to turn on the heat and told me to sit inside while he gathered our stuff, placing it in the trunk.

Once in the car, he turned to me and asked, "Are you warm enough?" I nodded. "Good. I want to take you one more place before lunch, if that's okay."

"Where?"

He grinned with his signature smile that always made my skin tingle. "It's a surprise."

Levi drove us to our old elementary school and parked in the parking lot. "Why are we here?"

"I want to show you something. Can you stand the cold for a little while longer?" I said I could because I was curious about his plan.

Helping me out of the car, he led me by the hand to the old oak tree where we had our first wedding in elementary school. My stomach was tied in knots, and, despite the cold, I started to sweat.

Levi got out his phone, set it up on one of the nearby benches, and started recording a video. I opened my mouth to protest, not wanting to be filmed again. But when I turned around to tell him, Levi dropped to one knee in front of me. He pulled out a small ring box and flashed a beautiful jade ring inside.

"Elle, I didn't do this right the first time. I was rash and made it seem like a joke, but I truly wanted to marry you then. I have since that day of our first wedding, and I still do and will every day for the rest of our lives. I wanted to ask you, formally, if you would do me the honor of continuing to be my wife."

I was nodding through tears, unable to speak, as he took off my glove and slipped the ring on my finger. We grabbed onto each other and began pressing our lips together repeatedly, not even matching up at times. With his gloved hands, he wiped the tears from my cheeks. They were almost frozen.

"Can, can I have your penis now?"

Levi threw his head back and laughed. "It'll shrivel up in this weather. I'll take us home."

Home. That sounded so comforting and rewarding. Like I had escaped my mother's dollhouse and could enjoy a new life with my husband where I was free.

I assumed he meant either my apartment or the TRZ manor. Maybe even my parent's house. Except for this time, we would be together. Instead, Levi drove us to an antique shop next to the bookstore on the main street in town and parked his car.

He got out and opened my door. "We're here."

Confused, I held his hand and walked with him toward the shop, but we diverted and went down a small alley to a bright blue door in the red brick wall. He reached into his pocket for a set of keys and unlocked it. Black-painted stairs led to another door off a landing.

Opening the door on the second floor, I was greeted by the smell of fresh paint and white walls in a sparsely furnished bright apartment. Levi threw the keys onto a console table by the entry and pulled me inside.

The living area had a worn green linen sofa with a red Persian rug underneath. A set of white plastic nesting tables sat in front as a coffee table. A large flat-screen TV sat on the floor across from the couch.

A small U-shaped kitchen was located to the right, with space for dining in between. There wasn't a table, but the kitchen had a countertop bar with two stools. Levi had bought new kitchen towels and placed them near the sink in a pile, tags still attached. A short hallway held two open doors. I assumed one was the bathroom and the other a bedroom.

"Welcome home." Levi looked nervous.

"Is this... is this *ours*?"

"I know it's not much, and I just got a few things because I figured we'd want to both fill it up. I only have a blow-up mattress right now and no pots or pans, but—"

"Levi, I love it!" I kissed him as he grabbed onto

me underneath my open coat. He stopped to take off our coats and throw them on the couch.

He pulled me around the apartment to show it off proudly, describing his visions of each space. "And here we could put one of those fake fireplaces, the kind that plugs in. That way, we can have stockings for Christmas. Here, the bathroom. Please put some wifey touches here. I don't know how to do that stuff. I just got one of those clear curtains for the shower."

Laughing at his excitement, I peered into each space and sharing his visions. I was high on happiness. The bathroom was a simple white tile floor and shower. There was a small linen closet and a medicine cabinet, with only two drawers under the sink. I'd have to pare down my toiletries, but I would have fun planning how to decorate our small space.

"Do you have bathroom towels?" I noticed there weren't any yet. At least there was toilet paper.

"Not yet. We can snag some from the manor. I was thinking we should have one of those fancy wedding receptions so we can get a bunch of gifted things for this place."

As he tugged my hand towards the last door, the large main bedroom spanned across the front of the building. There was a bay window overlooking the street. There was an air mattress, but a nice one that sat up off the floor. Levi had made up the bed with white sheets, blankets, and a ton of big pillows. It could have been in a nice hotel. There were candles on the packing crates next to the head of the bed and some tealights on the windowsills.

"Wait right there." He lit all the candles, and the room was bathed in dancing yellow light. Returning to me, he pressed his forehead to mine while stroking my hair. "Have you had enough time to date me?"

I laughed. "It will never be enough. I'm ready to be married to you."

"Good. Cause you are." His lips plunged into mine, tongue parting my mouth with fervent pressure. He unzipped my winter pants while I took off his hoodie, T-shirt, and base layers. He stripped me until we were naked, bodies pressed against each other for warmth. My soft curves melted into his hardness, and he lifted me by my bum as I clung to him.

He moved us over to the mattress and sat me down but quickly moved, so his head was near the foot of the bed, lying on his back. "Ride my face, hotness. I'm so hungry for your pussy." I kneeled over his head as he licked up my slit once, testing me. As I settled in, I squeezed my thighs around him, grinding down into his tongue and nose. He grasped my ass cheek with one hand and stroked his rock-hard cock with the other.

As he hardened his tongue and plunged, fucking me in my cunt, I came hard all over his face. I slowed my writhing hips as he licked up all my juices. "I need your penis," I panted out. The orgasm just wasn't as satisfying without it.

"Yes, ma'am." I dismounted, and he dragged me by the legs until I was face down on the airbed, head towards the end. He straddled my hips, my legs together, and slowly pushed his thick dick inside my wetness. From this angle, Levi was deeply embedded within me.

As soon as he was fully ensheathed, he grasped my hair in one hand. He pumped into me vigorously and pulled my head back at such an angle that he could lean over and kiss my lips. We continued making love like that, fully connected, body and soul.

Letting my head back down, he spanked me hard on the ass, and I jerked. "Fuck, your cunt clenches me when I do that. Keep doing it." He spanked me again, and I gasped. He started to spank me more until I felt myself escalating toward euphoria. The orgasm lasted longer than my typical ones. Each time his cock plied my pussy apart, it would pulsate harder as I arched my back and screamed his name.

Levi fell forward, his chest resting completely resting on my back. He wrapped his arms around me so he held my neck and hair, clutching my face to his. "You're addicted to this cock, aren't you." I whimpered in agreement as he stuck his tongue in my mouth. "Good, 'cause it craves your pussy. It's sleeping inside you tonight and every night. You'll wake up with me filling you up. You'll miss the feel of me when I'm not there." He continued to hump me closely, his hips jutting up and down rapidly until I could feel he was getting close. "I love you, dollface." His cock started throbbing inside of me and stuffing me with cum as he grunted loudly against my face.

He fully collapsed on top of me until I almost couldn't breathe, then rolled some to the side while panting heavily. We lay there together, gazing at each other in a stupor. Eventually, the feeling started coming back to me beneath my waist.

"It's cold!" I yelled and scrambled up to the head of the bed and got under the big blanket. He joined me.

"We'll have to get a space heater. Here." He grabbed my body, and we spooned for warmth.

"I can't leave the bed when it's this cold."

He laughed. "Not a problem. I'll get some soup delivered to us. No pots and pans yet, remember?" He grabbed his phone and ordered us some food for delivery.

"Levi?"

"Yes, wife?" After setting his phone down on the crate next to the bed, he turned back to spoon me.

"Do you want children?"

"Like just now? Like, did I just knock you up?" His face found mine with an expression of shock. He settled back against his pillow. "Sure, absolutely."

"No, not now. Just one day."

"If you do, yes. Whenever." Levi paused and furrowed his brow, chewing his lip. "Yeah. I hadn't thought about it seriously, but yes. I want a family.

Elle, I want to do it different than my parents. Or your mom. I want to have a stable family. And I think we can do that together. I can't do it alone. I need you."

I flipped around to smile at him and brushed one of his wavy locks off his forehead. "I'll be here."

"Okay, since you asked, I'm ready to make a baby now. Let's go." He growled and rolled on top of me.

"I'm on the pill." I laughed.

But that didn't stop him from trying. We fucked until the food arrived, then hopped in the shower to do it some more. He brought me a smaller blanket to dry off my body before he used it to dry his. Towels would be first on our list of goods to buy. Then, pots and pans.

That evening, we ended up "watching a movie" on the sofa but fucked on it instead. "Gotta hit all the rooms in here," Levi said.

"I'm sore," I replied while eating microwave popcorn. Levi scurried to the bedroom naked. He returned with the pillows and blanket off the bed.

"Okay, let's actually try to watch the movie now." He smiled. We cozied up together for warmth. A space heater was the third thing on the list, or the fake fireplace like my husband wanted. "We have one more room to fuck in. But it could wait until tomorrow." His arms tightened around me.

"We also have the next day, or the next day, or the next day, or the day after that until forever." I said, almost meeting his lips when I turned my head to him.

Levi grabbed the popcorn from me, threw it on the other side of the couch, kernels exploding everywhere. He leaned over me and kissed my lips passionately.

"Forever," he said.

epilogue

ELLE

"Little more to the left." I knew our friends were irritated with me, but I didn't care. "Yep, right there. Could you turn it? I want it at an angle." It was my first apartment with my husband; I wanted to make everything perfect. I had never decorated my own place before, just my dorm rooms or the small apartment bedroom. Levi was just as excited as I was.

The week before, I received my first paycheck from my new job post-graduation. Levi and I could finally start furnishing our place the way we wanted, with grown-up furniture. I was working in public relations for a local hospital. Levi was in his second year of MBA classes at night while working for my father during the day. His trades were going well, and he already had a few high-level clients. I was so proud of him.

We didn't have much, but I loved to hunt the sales and find the perfect furniture pieces for each room in our home. The antique shop below us had some great finds, which was why when I saw the heavy chifferobe at a discount price, I couldn't resist. Big G and Levi were trying to fit it into the right spot in our bedroom. Our closets were small, so the chifferobe would be able to fit more of my clothes.

We had added furniture to the living room, finding perfect comfy chairs and a loveseat. Our room had an actual bed now, with a metal rail headboard that made it great for gripping while riding Levi's cock. The kitchen and dining room were filled with items from our wedding reception held over a year ago for our first anniversary.

The Joseph Townsend Wedding was *the* event of the fall held at the Merrick country club. Millie Cardell planned the entire thing, which forced my mother to get her Botox injections early since she wasn't allowed to be involved. Levi nor I cared about the party as much as the presents and being able to hang out with our friends over expensive drinks, paid for by my generous father.

Levi's father had not been invited. The rumor among the elite of our community was that he and Levi had a rift over Levi's chosen employer. No one knew about Warren's extracurricular activities. And he had not tried to contact either of us since the altercation at the Cardell's holiday party.

"Just remember... pizza and beer," I said encouragingly to Big G and my husband.

"Huh. Not enough payment." We all paused as George spoke. I don't think I'd ever heard him say a full sentence. "But okay," he finished with a boom of his bass voice.

"Awesome. I'll grab you a beer." I walked towards the kitchen, stunned as Levi came up behind me.

"Did you just hear him?" Levi followed me. His eyes were wide.

"Yeah. I got scared," I confessed.

"See, told you. I thought I almost lost my dick that one time." Levi glanced down the hall to check that his friend hadn't heard us. "I'll grab those." He took the beer and a few slices of pizza to Big G as the big man adjusted the chifferobe angle.

Xavier and Mason walked in our open front door with Marissa and Kinsley. All were carrying boxes. Now that I had earned my first paycheck, I'd spent it on some essentials. Our friends were bringing in things from our wedding reception that I'd kept in storage until we had furniture to store them in. Everyone had been so lavish with their gifts. We were able to get almost everything we needed to outfit our apartment.

"If we ever move, you're helping us," Marissa said, taking a box of fancy dishes to the new dining area sideboard.

"We're not moving," Xavier told her firmly.

"I said *if*. I'd never want to." She smiled and kissed him lightly. They had a beautiful cabin on the lake that we loved to visit when we could.

"Do you guys want to play some board games or cards while we eat the pizza?" I started to bring out some from one of the boxes on the living room floor.

"Mrs. Cardell has had enough today. I'm taking her home," Xavier said emphatically, gripping Marissa's hand and shuffling her towards the door. I knew what that meant.

Levi ran to them from down the hall before they could leave. He said, "Hey. Thank you." He patted Xavier on the back.

I hugged Marissa. "Thank you guys so much. I'll babysit Ryan anytime." Their firstborn son was adorable, and I loved spending time with him when we got a chance. The four of us had become closer over the last year.

Turned out that Xavier wasn't a bully. Some part of me wondered if he had been an invisible hand leading Levi to me. He only liked a few people. Mainly just Marissa, but my husband was his other person. So that made Xavier my person, too.

"Sorry, I would stay to play, but you know how he gets." Marissa pointed at her husband, who fully yanked her out the door. Xavier's never-ending desire for her was legendary. I understood because my husband's libido was just as high.

"Where's my 'thank you'?" George said, walking

in from the hall, causing us all to jump. Kinsley rubbed his back.

"Damn, Kins. I don't know what you did to him. But I kind of liked the old, quiet G," Mason said. I grabbed a nearby pillow from a chair and threw it at him.

"I appreciate you, G. Thank you for helping me," I told him. "Games?" I asked again.

"We are also going to head out. George needs his neck massaged," Kinsley said with a twinkle in her eye, and he peered down at her as if he understood some secret hint.

"His penis neck?" Mason asked.

"Stop it, Locke," Kinsley scolded. "We will do games night soon, though," she said to me.

"See you guys." Levi came up behind me and put his arms around my waist. He lightly kissed my neck.

It was too much to assume Mason would take the hint. He sat on our couch and put his feet on the new coffee table, grabbing a slice of pizza and finishing his beer. Flipping the channels on the television, it was clear he was settled in for the evening.

"Um, Locke, buddy. How's it going?" Levi swayed with me in his arms, then pushed his growing erection into my back with urgency.

"S'good. You got any pepperoncini peppers? I like those with my pizza." He looked in the almost empty box.

"Mason, we need to get you a girlfriend... Or boyfriend?" I asked him.

Mason said dryly, "Girlfriend." He munched some more on his pizza. "I started seeing someone."

"Oh, that's good. Where is she?" I asked. Levi was growing impatient and hummed in my ear.

"Uh... she's out. She lives in a different town. You probably don't know her."

"Great, we will meet her sometime. See ya, Locke. Thanks for stopping by," Levi said. I swatted his hand with mine.

"Where does she live?" I asked to be polite.

Mason hadn't been one for keeping secrets, so he busted out like he'd been keeping hold of a good one for a while. "It's Whitney. I am fucking Whitney. And she's a bitch, I know this, but I don't mind. She's bored with her boyfriend."

"*Dude!*" Levi said. "Your bad choice, man. Never mind about bringing her over. Her invitation is revoked."

"Figured you'd say that. I'm not sure I even like her, so that's fine. She lets me watch her and her boyfriend fuck sometimes before I can get in there."

I got nauseous, picturing my cousin having sex with her new boyfriend and then Mason.

Levi made a gagging sound, "Mason! What the fuck, dude. Have some respect for yourself." He wandered away to get another beer.

"Oh, Mason. We can find you someone better." I

sat next to him and patted him on the back. "Someone who deserves you."

"No, we can't. Locke, time to get up and leave. Go fuck Whitney. You can't watch me fuck my wife."

"Fine, fine." Mason gathered up his stuff. "Thanks for inviting me." He walked out the front door, and Levi quickly threw the locks.

"Ugh, not sure why we're still friends with that guy. I know he's Xavier's family, but come on."

"Oh, be nice. He's seen all his friends pair up recently. I'm sure he's just lonely."

"Well, so am I... come here." Levi ran over to me, scooping me up in his arms, and carried me to the bedroom. "Finally... alone!"

epilogue

LEVI

Some days I missed our first apartment above the antique shop. It was quaint and quiet, just the two of us fucking any time we liked. We thought we were so busy then but didn't know the word's meaning. Today was one of those days I wanted to close my eyes and envision sitting on the crappy green couch while Elle sucked my cock.

My daughter was screaming because we'd kept her awake for her first birthday party so she could eat the chocolate cake I'd made. I didn't blame her; it wasn't a very good cake.

"Amelia, you don't have to eat it." I picked her up from the highchair, stroking her blond hair. There was a time when I could rock her back and forth, and she would quiet down. Now nothing seemed to make her settle, except for Grandpa. Where was he?

Elle's family was attending and "helping" to coordinate everything while Amelia's little cousins ran around, causing more chaos. Our new house was a wreck. Both my job and Elle's kept us busy, and we didn't care if it was straightened up or not. When we were here, we spent time as a family, not cleaning. This was home. It was comfortable, and it was ours.

"I got her if you want to take a break." Elle came up and kissed me quickly, taking Amelia from my arms.

"No, I've got her. We're cool. She needs a nap."

"No, I've got her. Give her here," my father-in-law and boss interrupted and grabbed his favorite granddaughter. "I never get to see her as often as I like." That was a lie; Will saw her at least every other day. He took off to the living room rocking chair to read her favorite book.

"Thanks, Dad." I put my arm around my wife and kissed her temple.

"You're sure you want another one?" Elle whispered and smiled.

"Only if you do," I said into her face, but I did. I wanted ten more. I loved being a dad.

She sighed, "Yep. I do. I want more. In probably another year, though."

I laughed. "Whenever, as long as we keep practicing."

"As soon as they all leave, I'm down for practicing."

"Okay, everyone out! Party's over!" I yelled, and

Elle tried to shush me, pulling my arms down and laughing.

I still didn't get along with Veronica Townsend. Probably never would, but we tolerated each other. She was in the kitchen with Elle's sisters, judging our house.

Elle's brothers-in-law, Will, and I had formed a massive male alliance to overrule Veronica's controlling ways. She had less power when we stood as a united front. Will had changed over the years, and she seemed more deferential to his desires now. I figured he got tired of her bullshit now that it was just the two of them at their house. It didn't make Elle's sisters any more tolerable, but at least all of us guys could commiserate with each other at family functions.

Since I started working for him, Will transitioned from friend to advisor to genuine father figure and much less of a boss. I think he wanted me to take over the company someday. He inspired me so much that I aspired to do so. We would joke that the company would change its name to Joseph-Townsend Financials, but Will wasn't kidding when he said it.

Elle enjoyed doing public relations for one of the main hospitals in the area. She was fantastic at her job, and I was always impressed whenever I got to show Amelia her mother on TV. Since college, we never saw another copy of our exposed video online. We'd done a good job distancing ourselves from that fiasco... and my father.

Father and I were civil to each other, but there was no warmth between us. Whenever we spoke, it was only about business; I was happy with that. He was not allowed near our daughter or Elle. He had never been to our home. Warren remained a bachelor, alone in his stone castle.

My mother and I had made up enough that she was invited to family holidays and Amelia's birthday party. She would bring her latest boyfriend, and I tried to ignore the disaster that was her love life. She genuinely tried to be a better grandmother than a mother; I respected that.

Adam, who was in the corner now with his wife, came with their kids. Xavier and Marissa and their brood also showed up. Our other couples' friends all arrived with their children. Things were chaotic for a child's birthday party. I'd dreamed of having a family, and now I did. The first year of Amelia's life had been tough, but the hard work was worth it. I loved my life.

Adam approached Elle and me. "I'll pay you guys to take our kids the rest of the weekend. They need time with Uncle Levi and Auntie Elle."

"No. Absolutely no way." I shoved his shoulder with mine. We had grown closer than ever over the last few years. We had become true brothers. Adam still communicated with Warren, but he was good about letting my father and I keep things icy without trying to push for anything more. He'd stopped playing mediator and let us have it out between ourselves.

Xavier heard us talking and strolled over. "We'll take them all. I can't wait for Marissa to spit this one out so I can put another in her." Man was a sadist.

Elle huffed, then left to commiserate with a pregnant Marissa and the other wives.

"You need to slow down. Save some sperm for the rest of the world," I told him. Xavier continued to wax poetically about his lake life in their cabin. We made plans to go fishing in the coming weeks with Dad (Will) and Mason.

Mine and Elle's anniversary was approaching, and I had secretly gotten my wife a gift I knew she'd love. Watching her talk with her friends, she flirted with me with her eyes. It spurred me into action. "I'll be back," I told Xavier and Adam.

I walked over to the gals and grabbed Elle by the hand. "What are you doing?"

"Come here." I pulled her into my lower-level office and pushed her against the wall as I shut and locked the door. It was finally quiet.

"We don't have time! We have guests!" I pushed my knee between her legs and sucked her neck, then nibbled down to her generous bosom. She moaned, "Yes, right there."

"Mmm, dollface, I actually brought you in here to give you something."

"Give it to me, Daddy." My wife was truly addicted to my cock. She tried to wrap a leg around my waist.

"Not that... yet." I reached over to my desk and grabbed the envelope. I handed it to her.

"What's this?"

"Early anniversary present." I licked my lips as she opened it.

She gasped when she did, "Is this... a honeymoon to our resort? The one we got married at?"

I nodded. She jumped and wrapped her arms and legs around me. I held her, rocking back and forth. "I told you I'd marry you every day if I could. Is it a good present?"

"The absolute best!"

I kissed her deeply, then lifted her skirt and pushed her panties to the side so I could quickly thrust inside her. We had time. I finally got to kiss her whenever I wanted.

acknowledgments

To my friends and first readers. I can't thank you enough for your continued efforts to make me a good writer. To my husband, who gave me the courage to walk through my cage door. To my father, who will never, ever read this. Despite your flaws, you have given me creativity and courage. Without you, I wouldn't be where I am today.

To Sarah, my editor, who taught me so much along the process of writing correctly. The lesson I learned is, always, add, more, commas.

To every service worker ever at any all-inclusive I have ever stayed at. You the real MVPs. Thanks for always serving up amazing fruity drinks just when I need it.

about the author

Kitty King is a romance writer by day and a psychiatrist by night. She is the author of the number one bestselling new release in romantic erotica, *Red Night: Xavier's Delight*. Kitty enjoys reading erotic romance tales just as much as writing them. Besides reading and writing, she spends her spare time hiking with her husband and playing with her overzealous dogs. She is often known for inputting rare *Buffy the Vampire Slayer* quotes into everyday language and being overly competitive in hidden identity boardgames.

http://authorkittyking.com

also by kitty king

THE COLOR SERIES

Red Night: Xavier's Delight (Book 1)

Blue Film (Book 2)

White Hole (Book 3)

STANDALONE

The Wrong Man

Full list on Amazon author's page:

http://amazon.com/author/kittykingauthor

next in the series...

What happened with Big G and Kinsley?

Want in on the action during the foursome with Levi, Xavier, G's stepmother, and stepsister?

Check out *White Hole*, book 3 in The Color Series.

When the stars misalign... You have a big bang with your future ex-step mother-in-law

Kinsley

There's only one class that's been stopping me from my perfect grade point average... Astronomy. Nothing will stand in my way from getting an A, not even the tutor I've been assigned. George is arrogant, rude, and, confusingly, barely opens his mouth. How am I supposed to learn from someone who doesn't talk?

George

When the princess I saved last Friday night signs up for my tutoring sessions, I'm irritated. She's pretentious, draining, and, worst of all, won't shut up. How am I supposed to teach when she won't stop talking? When I find out that her past may cause my family problems... I know I need to avoid her. Right?

• Dark erotic romantic novel

• Enemies-to-lovers

• Dual POV

Made in the USA
Las Vegas, NV
22 December 2023